LONGARM C...

WHAT H...

His jaw dropped, and the Colt he'd whipped from its holster sagged in his hand as he stared at the boat and the crew manning it.

Bull Kestell, the double-barreled shotgun he'd fired still angled in his hands, was half standing, half crouching in the prow of an oversized rowboat. Four other men—loggers by the look of them—were also in the boat. Two manned the oars, a third was at the tiller, and another standing in the stern.

The man in the stern held a rifle, the menacing muzzle slowly traversing the shoreline as he sought a target. Longarm suddenly found himself looking down the black muzzle of the weapon and dropped to one knee.

Before the rifleman could squeeze off his shot, the bow of the boat caught on a submerged boulder, and the craft tilted precariously. The marksman had not yet found Longarm in his sights. His trigger-finger tightened involuntarily as the boat grated across the boulder.

Angrily the rifle barked.

Also in the LONGARM series
from Jove

TABOR EVANS

LONGARM

AND THE REDWOOD RAIDERS

JOVE BOOKS, NEW YORK

LONGARM AND THE REDWOOD RAIDERS

A Jove Book/published by arrangement with
the author

PRINTING HISTORY
Jove edition/December 1989

ISBN: 0-515-10193-1

LONGARM

AND THE
REDWOOD RAIDERS

Chapter 1

Longarm stopped when he'd reached the crest of the rise. He stood for a moment looking at the jagged rocky line that marked the crest of Berthoud Pass. It was at least two hundred yards ahead of him, the slope to its peak of saw-toothed stone just as steep and rocky as the one he'd just climbed. Beyond the uneven line where the rise ended there was another and another and still others, until at last only grey clouds were visible.

A light fine-flaked snow had started sifting down from the leaden sky more than an hour ago. When it began the tiny flakes had melted as soon as they had touched the ground, but as the wind grew colder and the sun moved down the western sky the flakes stayed intact. Now snow stood in thin patches that were slowly growing larger, the snow falling faster and the flakes bigger. The white blobs swirled in the steadily rising wind that had begun riffling downslope even before Longarm reached the bottom of the roughly bow-shaped slope of the pass.

1

Cradling his Winchester in the crook of his elbow, Longarm pushed one gloveless hand through the vee of his coat lapels and fumbled for a cheroot in his vest pocket while he studied the rise confronting him. His fingers were already so numb that he had to hold them against his chest for a moment to warm them before he could separate one of the long thin cigars from the half dozen his pocket held. He worked the cheroot free without breaking his observation of the slope and clamped the cigar in his strong teeth while he began trying to get a match from his lower vest pocket.

Succeeding at last, he drew his iron-hard thumbnail over the match head and puffed the cigar tip into a glowing goal before the swirling wind blew out the burning match.

"Well, old son," Longarm said aloud as he faced the chilling gusts that were sending sharp trickles of icy air through every small gap between the flaps of his coat, "looks like you got here in time. The snow ain't sticking much yet, but if that damn Clete Forson had passed this way, he'd've left some kinda sign on them ridges the snow's covered up ahead."

Reasonably certain now that he'd reached a strategic spot ahead of the fugitive killer, Longarm selected the nearest of the two possible hiding places his observation had revealed and struck out again, heading for it. The spot he'd chosen during his brief search was behind a split boulder that rose head-high beside the trail. The massive boulder was big enough to conceal him on either side of the jagged crack that had divided it, and that split was wide enough to give him space to swing the barrel of his rifle and cover the faintly beaten path that zigzagged upward in gentle sweeps.

Step by careful step, Longarm picked his way over the slanting, snow-slick broken terrain until he reached the boulder. He stepped behind it and surveyed the downslope.

2

It was still deserted, but he hadn't expected the fugitive killer to be very close behind him.

In fact, the biggest question of all remained unanswered, though Longarm had agreed with the suggestion made by Billy Vail in the telegram his chief had sent him from Denver. The wired orders postponed Longarm's return and noted Vail's hunch that the escaped murderer would head at once for the high country. The northern peaks of the Colorado Rockies rising in boundless loneliness were dotted with outlaw hideouts. In such a vast expanse there were scores of places for wanted men to make themselves scarce when the law was on their trail, and both Longarm and Vail knew the trails that led to most of the outlaw havens.

Vail's telegram had caught Longarm between trains in Boulder. He was waiting there for the southbound UP flyer to carry him on the last leg of his return to Denver, and had telegraphed his chief that he was on his way back after closing a case that had taken him to Colorado's western prairie country. The very fact that Billy Vail had thought it important enough to delay Longarm's return and request him to make such a special effort to recapture Clete Forson had set Longarm on his present search.

Vail, Longarm recalled at once, had a special reason for seeing that Forson was recaptured and brought to justice, for less than three months ago the outlaw had been captured by the chief marshal himself. Taking Forson prisoner was the climax of the running gun battle that had left Forson's sidekick dead and two of the Denver federal marshal's office deputies wounded.

Hunkering down behind the big split rock, Longarm settled into as comfortable a position as possible on the sharp broken stones that covered the ground. He was prepared to wait for a limited time, for if the outlaw had chosen this route to take to freedom, he'd be showing up soon.

If Forson failed to show up within the next half or three-quarters of an hour, it would mean one of two things. Either he'd been captured before reaching Berthoud Pass, or had struck out in a different direction in his effort to escape. The Rocky Mountain high country offered hundreds of places of concealment, and Longarm was gambling against short odds that the escaped outlaw wouldn't have chosen to risk crossing the relatively open eastern prairie. The gamble that the fugitive would choose the less risky and fairly plentiful escape routes through the Rockies was one which Longarm was prepared to take.

He'd waited almost three-quarters of an hour when the crunching sound of snow and rocks disturbed by boot soles was borne by the upslope breezes to Longarm's ears. If his attention had been lagging during the time he'd been waiting, that lapse had ended with the first noises. Longarm shifted his rifle into a position where he could shoulder it at once and sharpened his gaze on the now almost-invisible snow-pocked trail that ran up the slanting rocky ground.

After the first muffled sound of boot soles scraping rock, only a few minutes ticked away before Longarm got his first fleeting glimpse of the fugitive. Though he saw little more than the corner of a man's shoulder exposed behind a wide gap in the ridge below, Longarm was sure he'd hit pay dirt.

Keeping his eyes fixed on the now almost-obliterated trail below, he eased into a more comfortable position in his hiding place. By the time Longarm settled himself in an easier posture Forson had emerged into full view. The snowfall had not yet grown thick enough to obscure Longarm's vision, and he saw that in the relatively few hours that followed his escape the outlaw had somehow gotten hold of a rifle. He was moving fast, a sign that he felt secure on the slope, that he was certain he'd shaken off the

4

pursuers who Longarm knew would have started after him almost at once.

Moving slowly, Longarm returned his rifle to a position that would enable him to shoulder it instantly. Forson's speed and accuracy with both rifle and pistol were well known to every lawman who'd faced him. Longarm was well aware that in spite of his protected position he was still vulnerable to an expert shot, even though the snow was falling more heavily now in big flakes that seemed to form in midair and increase in size as they wafted to the rocky surface.

Somehow, perhaps guided by the sixth sense that outlaws are forced to acquire early in their lawless days in order to survive, Forson stopped and began searching the upslope with his eyes. Longarm's move in raising the muzzle of his Winchester had been enough to alert the fleeing gunman. Forson fired his rifle without shouldering it, shooting from the hip as though his weapon was a pistol.

Longarm's answering shot caught up the echoes of the round loosed by the fugitive. Forson's bullet shattered chips of rock from the long narrow vee where Longarm was standing. The spent slug sailed harmlessly past Longarm's shoulder while he was triggering his own Winchester, and as he tilted his head to shield his eyes from the rain of small stone chips, he saw Forson's body jerk as the lead from the Winchester went home.

It was not a fatal shot. Forson flinched but did not fall. Longarm crouched lower in order to shield himself more effectively. He'd already started moving when the outlaw's next slug whistled above his head and splatted with an angry thunk in the thin layer of dirt that covered the sheer rocky rise that stood behind Longarm's improvised bastion.

Raising his voice, Longarm called, "Give up, Forson! You already took one bullet and I guarantee you aren't going to come outa this alive if you play the fool and keep on shooting!"

Forson's only reply was another shot. Longarm had not been expecting any other response, and while he'd been ordering the outlaw to surrender he'd crouched even lower. Though the singing lead cut through the center of the boulder's crack, it passed above Longarm's head and the only damage it did was to the face of the sheer rise behind the boulder.

After he'd triggered off his reply to Longarm's call, Forson had dropped flat. Now Longarm could not see him, as ridges in the downslope between the two hid them from one another. Longarm did not make the mistake of underestimating his enemy's skill and cunning. He did not call to the fugitive outlaw a second time, but studied his position, looking for a way to bring Forson into his sights without exposing himself to the criminal's expert marksmanship. Knowing Forson's record, Longarm did not expect the outlaw to surrender or to retreat. He was sure that his antagonist was prepared to hold his position and fight it out.

"You're right in the middle of a Mexican standoff, old son," Longarm muttered in a thoughtful voice, speaking just above a whisper. "And damn near any move you make's likely to be the wrong one. But that mean-hearted bastard down there below doesn't have any more choice than you have. Whatever he does is bound to be a wrong move, too. Question is, which one of us is going to do the wrong thing first?"

A grating of loose rocks from the direction of Forson's position gave Longarm his answer almost at once. Disregarding the risk of exposing himself to a shot, he leaned to one side and peered through the cleft in the boulder. A suggestion of movement, a quick glimpse of what Longarm took to be his enemy's arm passing across the small area visible through the slit in the big rock, was his only reward. The single flash of motion he saw could have meant anything or nothing.

Though Longarm had learned from his many brushes with the lawless the need for expecting the unexpected, he was not prepared for the crack of Forson's rifle, or for the whistling chunk of hot lead that scored the massive rock wall behind him. He dropped to his knees as the slug screeched across the face of the impenetrable stone, leaving a jagged white scratch on its weather-beaten surface.

Longarm dropped flat when his quick backward glance revealed the line of chipped white. That single quick look told him that if he'd been leaning against the face of the stone cliff at his back the bullet would have certainly plowed through his chest or head. Rising on to his knees now, Longarm crawled on all fours back to his observation slit. This time he did not rise to look through the gap, but kept moving slowly on his hands and knees along the rounded base of the cracked boulder.

He inched past the jagged edged crack to where the space between the boulder and the sheer granite wall narrowed. There was not enough space for him to crawl on all fours. Longarm lay down on his side, clamped the butt of his rifle in his armpit, and began propelling himself ahead in his prone position. By stretching his arms ahead and groping at the base of the boulder until he found a crack or a projection that he could grasp, he began inching ahead.

He'd covered only a third of the distance to the edge of the crevice when Forson's rifle spoke again. Its slug scored a second line of white just below the first on the surface of the towering solid rock formation that Longarm had been depending on to shield his back.

"You lucked out twice now, old son," Longarm muttered as he glanced at the evidence of the bullets that solely by chance had missed him. "And that sharpshooting son of a bitch out there ain't about to stop trying. But sooner or later he's going to start feeling just a mite too free, and that's when he's likely to get careless. All you got to do is find the right spot and wait and be ready."

Still stretched on his side in the cramped space of the narrow cleft, he continued to worm his way inch by inch along the base of the huge cracked boulder. The pebbles and rocks that filled the gap between the solidly sheer back wall of the crevice and the bottom of the rounded boulder poked painfully into his ribs and forearms and gouged at his thighs as he dragged himself along a few inches at a time. In spite of the scraping, Longarm persisted.

He reached the end of the boulder. Its narrowing rounded edge slanted into the ground, creating a lopsided triangle between the thin rock-studded soil and the bulge of the big monolith that rose above it. The opening was not large, but by leaning forward and stretching his head to the utmost Longarm could get a clear view of the steep slope that fell away from the massive granite formation.

Only the boles of a few spindling stunted pine trees broke the line of sight along the steep slope. Longarm scanned the ground carefully. For several moments he saw no sign of motion anywhere in his restricted vista, which was boulder studded over most of its barren expanse. Then he caught sight of a flick of motion between a group of the boulders that were strewn across the long barren expanse that dipped downward.

Longarm worked his Winchester free and with slow careful moves placed it where he could shoulder the weapon. He kept his eyes on the spot where he'd seen movement, and after what seemed a long wait Forson's head and shoulders came into view as the escaped outlaw inched out of the hiding place that the scattered boulders had created. He was pushing his rifle ahead of him, and left the weapon lying on the ground while he got to his feet.

Now Longarm had a clear field of vision and was holding Forson in his sights. Although he was tempted to shoot, his lawman's code was too strong to allow him to close his finger on the Winchester's trigger. Duty required him to give even a killer a chance to surrender.

"Forson!" he called. "Freeze right there! I got you cold! If you make one move to draw or grab up your rifle, I'll pull the trigger on you!"

At the first sound of Longarm's voice, Forson had dropped to his knees and reached for his rifle. Longarm had no choice. He had the outlaw in his sights and shifted his aim for a shot that would wound rather than kill. Forson had just succeeded in closing his hand around his rifle's stock when Longarm's lead tore into his upper arm and knocked him backward. He laid prone, half stunned by the bullet's smashing impact.

Longarm raced to the outlaw and kicked the butt of the rifle to put it beyond his reach, then planted a boot sole firmly on Forson's uninjured arm while he bent down to yank the man's pistol from its holster. Forson was beginning to moan softly as the first nerve-shattering shock of the rifle slug diminished and he began to feel the pain of his wounded shoulder traveling down along his arm.

"Damn you, Long!" he grated. "Another hour or so and I'd've been clear gone! How in hell did you get after me so fast, anyhow?"

"I'll leave you to worry about that," Longarm said. There was no sympathy in his voice. He went on, "If you'd been smart enough to give up like I told you to do, you wouldn't be hurting now. Seeing as you wasn't all that bright, I got to get you bandaged up before you bleed to death. Soon as I do, we'll start for Boulder, then catch a train to Denver and the jail doctor can bandage you proper."

"You mean I got to walk all the way down this mountain, all shot up and bleeding like I am?" Forson protested.

"Walk or crawl, or I'll drag you if it comes to that. Now stop your bellyaching and I'll see what I can do to fix up your arm before we head out for Boulder."

"You know, Billy, I wouldn't mind a bit if you'd let me wind up one case before you sent me out on the next one," Longarm said as he stepped into Vail's office in the Denver Federal Building the next morning. "I guess you got the telegram I sent you from Boulder last night?"

"I just finished reading it," Vail said.

Ignoring his chief's remark, Longarm went on, "I ain't much of a one to complain, Billy, but I had to take that damn Forson fellow to the hospital and wait while they bandaged him up, then I had to take him to the jail. Damn it, I ain't even had breakfast yet, and here it is close to the middle of the day!"

"You're the one who shot him," Vail pointed out.

"Sure. Just in time to keep him from shooting me. And I got him bandaged up so he wouldn't bleed to death, too. But there wasn't time before the train left from Boulder for me to take him to a doctor and get him fixed up proper. I just got away from that hospital, Billy, and like I said, I ain't even had my breakfast yet."

"If you can listen to me for a few more minutes without starving, I'll tell you something that you can chew on with your breakfast," Vail said.

"Oh, I can hold out a little while longer."

A smile crossed Vail's face as he went on, "If it'll make you feel any better, in my next report to Washington I'm putting you up for a special merit bonus because of the way you handled that case and brought Forson in before he'd been loose more than a few hours."

For a moment Longarm stared, speechless, then he said, "I don't remember you ever done that more'n about three times in all the years I've been working for you, Billy."

"That's because the big brass in Washington doesn't really like those bonus awards," Vail replied. "And I'd say it'll be a good idea if you wait till you've got the voucher in your hand before you start out to spend it. Remember, they might not approve my recommendation in Washington."

"I'll take the will for the deed," Longarm said promptly. "And I thank you kindly for doing it, whether I get a dime of the bonus or not."

"Well, you earned it," Vail replied. "But don't look for the money to be coming in before you start out to take care of the new case you're going out on."

"I should've known there'd be a catch to it," Longarm said. "I just hope you ain't sending me to the North Pole or someplace like that."

"Not exactly to the North Pole." Vail smiled. "Just to the northern part of California."

"But, Billy, that's a good far piece outside of our district! What in tunket's happened out there that concerns us?"

"Not all of it's happened yet, that's one reason you're going to California, to keep trouble from starting."

"Now you're talking riddles again. Maybe you better start at the beginning and tell me what I'm about to run into."

Vail picked up a telegram flimsy from his littered desktop and handed it to Longarm. In the round Spencerian script that he recognized as being that of the head telegrapher stationed in the Denver Federal Building basement,

Longarm read, *Order D-65837. Immediate execution upon receipt. Deputy Marshal Custis Long on detached duty from Denver office as of current date. Deputy Long to report to Chief, Indian Bureau Western Headquarters San Francisco for immediate special assignment per Indian Bureau request. Acknowledge departure date on receipt.*

Chapter 2

"It's sure good to see things ain't no different from the way they've always been in Washington," Longarm said dryly after he'd read the wire. "Them fellows back East don't believe in giving a man much elbow room, do they?"

"They never have before," Vail replied, "so I don't imagine they're likely to start now."

"If I have to hit the road again, I guess you figure to let me have a little time to get ready," Longarm went on. "I need to get my laundry done, and there's a few other little chores to take care of, like buying some new socks. Every pair I have now is so holey that old Saint Peter'd let 'em come right through the pearly gates without making any fuss."

"I'm sure the Indian Bureau brass won't be expecting you to report to San Francisco tomorrow," Vail allowed. "There's not any real hurry. If you need a little time, go ahead and take it. Remember, it's likely you'll be out on the West Coast for quite a spell."

13

"It ain't going to take me all that long to get ready to travel again, Billy," Longarm assured his chief. He handed the telegram flimsy back to Vail. "Not more than a day or so."

"That'll be fine," Vail said with a nod as he took the flimsy. He opened the drawer of his desk and started to put the telegram away, then shook his head. Taking an envelope from the drawer he held it out to Longarm and went on, "I must be getting old, if forgetting things is a sign. This letter came in a couple of days ago and I tucked it away until you got back."

Longarm had already recognized the familiar grey envelope with its engraved monogram of entertwined letters on the flap. He took it from Vail without comment and slipped it into his pocket.

"Thanks, Billy. This can wait till after breakfast, and I'm way past due for some grub. Let's go hang on the feedbag. We can hash over that new business about me going out to California while we're taking on a load of bacon and eggs. And maybe a stack of hotcakes, too, the way my stomach feels right now."

Pushing away his empty plate Longarm looked across the table at Vail. The two men had talked little during the meal, most of the conversation concentrated on the details of the speed with which Longarm had intercepted and re-captured Clete Forson.

Vail was draining the last dregs of coffee from his cup. He swallowed and said, "If you're interested in hearing what I've figured is responsible for the Indian Bureau wanting you to go to the West Coast, it was the job you did when you cleaned out that gang of crooked Indian agents over in the Nation a while back."

"Shucks, Billy! I didn't do it all by myself. I had that little Ponca girl to tell me all about the thieving them crooked agents was doing, and she showed me the lay of the land and all. I got to give her most of the credit."

"I don't recall running across her name in your reports," the chief marshal said, frowning.

"There's crooks in the Indian Bureau in Washington, just like there were in the Indian Nation. I wasn't about to give them a line on her. They'd've found a way to get back at her, maybe even to kill her."

Vail nodded slowly. "That makes sense." Pushing his chair back from the table he went on as he stood up, "I hope you have as good luck on this new job the Indian Bureau's asked for you to handle. Now, I've got to get back to the office. Suppose you take the rest of the morning off. You said you needed a little time to get a spare pair of socks or something like that before you leave."

"I do, Billy. But I need an hour or so of shut-eye first. I sure didn't get a lot of sleep last night, having to keep an eye on that Forson rascal."

"Don't be in a hurry, then. When you come in later on we'll sit down and figure out whatever details we can about you tying up loose ends you've got here before you leave."

Vail had not reached the door to the street before Longarm was digging in his pocket for the letter from Julia Burnside. He ripped its flap open and unfolded the single folded sheet of stationery it contained.

Longarm, my dear, he read in Julia Burnside's bold sprawling handwriting. *Let's try again and hope our luck is better than it was when I last passed through Denver several months ago and failed to see you. I must go to the West Coast again, and on this trip my car will be attached to the Limited arriving in Denver on morning of the 17th. I'm afraid my situation this time is the same, though. Much as I'd like to, I can't stop over. Even a few minutes will be wonderful, so even if we can only have a quick visit I'll be looking for you at the depot. Love, Julia.*

Longarm refolded the letter, and as he returned it to his pocket he suddenly realized that during the busy time that had just ended he'd lost track of the days. He glanced around the restaurant, looking for a calendar, but saw none. Standing up, he hurried back to the Federal Building. The door to Vail's private office was open. The chief marshal frowned when he saw Longarm and called to him.

"I thought I gave you the rest of the morning off," he said as Longarm came into his office. "If you're looking for your expense vouchers and travel orders, they're not ready yet and won't be until tomorrow. Didn't I mention that?"

"You did, Billy, and I plumb forgot it. Damn it, a man that's been moving around fast as I have on such short notice can't be expected to remember everything. I just sorta lost track of what day of the month it is and this was the closest place where I was sure I'd find a calendar."

"There it is," Vail told him, gesturing at the calendar on his office wall. "The fifteenth. Why? Did you forget what day payday is, or is it some woman that's expecting you to drop in on her?"

"You know I'd remember if it was either one of them things. I just got to thinking about what you said while we were eating, and figured I better know whether tomorrow's Monday or Saturday or some day in between."

"Well, you can see for yourself easily enough. It's the fifteenth of the month, which happens to fall on Tuesday."

"Damn it, I ain't forgot how to read! But now that I know, I might as well tell you that Thursday's as good a day as any for me to start out. That'll be the seventeenth."

"Fine. And if you've finished giving me my arithmetic lesson, I'll look for you to come back later on for our confab."

During the time before his meeting with Vail, Longarm cured the shortcomings of his wardrobe and spent a luxurious half hour in a Turkish bath, sweating the strains of the last few busy days out of his muscles. After another half hour, this one in a barber's chair, he strode into the office with his cheeks smooth and redolent of bay rum from his recent shave, and his shock of brown hair neatly combed.

"Now then, Billy," he said to Vail, "what all else have I got to take care of besides the job the Indian Bureau's putting me on?"

"Damn little," Vail replied. "There's only outlaws we told Washington we'd keep an eye out for, and I've got a hunch that the man we're looking for on one of them has gone and gotten himself killed while he was using another name."

"That'd be Fletcher? The one that calls hisself Grizzly Pete?"

Vail nodded. "He's either dead or he's moved out of our district. You might run into him in California, though. That seems to be where the roughest characters are heading these days. There, and getting out of our jurisdiction by moving up to Canada."

"Don't worry about me forgetting Grizzly Pete, Billy. I still got him on my list. Now, who else is there on yours?"

"Jim McKinney. Folks from up in his hometown have been whispering that somebody recognized him out in California. It might be just a lot of talk, but since you'll likely be rambling around at least a little bit, you might cross his trail."

"I'll know him if I see him," Longarm promised. "I've sure seen his picture enough."

"Well, those two seem to be the only ones on my list that were likely to push as far as California. That's a funny thing I've noticed about outlaws, they like to stick close to home."

"Sure. That's where folks live who'll give 'em a hidey-hole and whatever grub they need. But now that I've got your list, Billy, I don't see much reason to come back today, if it's all right with you. We got all day tomorrow to finish our palaver."

"And I've got a desktop full of work to take care of," Vail said, grimacing. "Go on about your business. Just come in on time tomorrow, and we'll get you your vouchers."

Longarm knew the instant he woke up the following morning that during the night while he'd been sleeping the weather had been changing. The cracks in the aging roller shade that covered the window across from his bed were barely visible against the dim light outside, appearing as thin white lines instead of glowing gold from a rising sun. Even indoors the air was chilly. He reached for the shirt that hung over the back of the chair beside his bed and slid his arms into the sleeves before lighting his first cigar of the day.

"Old son, it looks like you're going to get outa Denver just in time, if the middle of this snowstorm don't move in too fast," he said. In the cold silent air his voice was flat. "California's likely to be a pretty good place to go to if Denver's gonna be hit by one of them big wet blowups."

Reluctantly, Longarm climbed fully out of bed. A splash of cold water on his face from the bowl on his nightstand got his eyes wide open in a hurry, and after drawing a time or two on his fresh cigar he made short work of pulling on his jeans and stepping into his boots. After strapping on his gun belt and shrugging into his long-skirted bad-weather coat he set his hat in place and started down the stairway to the front door.

If the thin trickles of air that invaded his room had seemed cold, the chill was nothing compared to the sweeping gusts that greeted him when Longarm opened the front door and started toward Cherry Creek. Two inches of snow

18

already covered the ground, and by the time he'd crossed the Colfax Avenue bridge and turned toward Denver's downtown district the air was filled with big swirling flakes sifting down thickly enough to hide the golden dome of the Colorado state capitol.

By the time Longarm stepped into the office, the morning assignment rush had passed and the daily messages from Washington had been delivered from the basement telegraph room. The young pink-cheeked clerk was bent over his desk, leafing through a two-inch-high stack of telegraph-paper flimsies, and barely nodded as Longarm passed him with a gesture of greeting. The door to Billy Vail's office was ajar and he could see the chief marshal thumbing through another equally thick sheaf of the thin yellow paper.

"If you've come to get your travel orders and vouchers, Henry's got them ready for you," Vail said, looking up from his desk as Longarm entered. "And I haven't gone through all this mess of stuff from headquarters yet, but there's not likely to be anything new in it that'd concern what you'll be doing when you get to California."

"You know what that sounds like to me, Billy? I got a hunch you're telling me to take a day off."

"Now, you've been working here long enough to know that's not department policy," Vail said. There was a smile on his face that did not match the stern tone of his voice. "But even if I started you out on a new case today, you'd be leaving before you'd have time to do any real work on it."

"You know how I feel about just keeping a chair warm, Billy," Longarm said. "And I guess I got enough sense to take a hint. I'll pick up my papers, then, and you won't see hide nor hair of me till this Indian Bureau job's done."

"Fine," Vail agreed. "We'll leave it at that and I'll be sure to see you've got a case to keep you busy when you get back from taming the Indians out in California."

So many months had passed since he'd last been at loose ends that Longarm had a bit of trouble accepting the fact that for an entire day and night he was free to do whatever he wanted to. Taking the thick envelope Henry handed him, he tucked it into the inside breast pocket of his coat and descended the stairs to the street.

Longarm glanced up at the dark grey clouds, which were still shedding their leaden snow. The lowering sky, combined with the plucking of an icy, whistling wind, threw the flakes downward to add to the accumulation covering the streets in all directions, convincing Longarm that this weather would do nothing to make his unexpected day off enjoyable.

He ticked off in his mind the list of small chores that would require his attention before stepping on the westbound train the following day. Then he thought of the days that he and Julia would share on the long trip west. After a meditative moment he started down Champa Street, walking unhurriedly toward the Colfax Avenue bridge and his rooming house.

"Longarm!" Julia Burnside exclaimed as she opened the door of her private car. "I've been looking for you along the platform ever since we pulled in. When I didn't see you, I was afraid you were out of town on a case and hadn't gotten my letter."

Longarm was looking at her without trying to hide his admiration. He could see no change since their last brief meeting. Her dark eyes were glowing, her generous red lips spread in a happy smile to reveal a line of perfect white teeth. The lounging robe she wore was a soft blue silk that clung to her full, high-standing breasts and statuesque figure.

"I got on board up at the head of the train," Longarm replied at last. "You see, I—"

"Tell me later," Julia broke in.

She took Longarm's hand and drew him into the car, then closed the door before throwing her arms around him and turning her face up for his kiss. They held their embrace until the sharp tooting of the train's whistle reached their ears.

"Oh, damn!" Julia burst out as she relaxed her arms and took a half step backward. "The train's ready to move and we haven't even had time to look at one another!"

"There's something I ain't had a chance to tell you yet," Longarm said. "I'm heading for California, just like you are."

"Does that mean you're not going to be stationed in Denver any longer?"

"Not by a long shot. The Indian Bureau asked for me to take care of a case they got out there."

"And you'll be traveling on this train?"

"I sure will. All the way to San Francisco."

"Then you'll have to stay with me, here in my car!"

"I was sorta hoping you'd say that."

"You knew quite well I would!" Julia smiled. Suddenly the car lurched as the locomotive took up slack, then with a squeal of wheels on rails it began to move slowly forward. "I hope you brought your luggage aboard."

"It's out in the vestibule."

"Bring it in here, then. As soon as you do that, I'll put my DO NOT DISTURB sign on the door and lock it. This trip will be the first time in far too long that we've had more than a few hours together, and I intend to make the most of it."

Longarm traveled light, as was his habit. He took time to discard his heavy coat, then brought his saddlebags and rifle into the stateroom. Julia was standing at a small table

21

at the rear of the coach's sitting room, opening a bottle of champagne.

"I thought we ought to have a little celebration," she said. "Our reunions have been so far apart that they need to be observed properly." She handed him one of the glasses filled with the golden, foam-topped wine. Then she raised her own glass and said, "To being together, Longarm."

"I'll sure drink to that with you," he replied.

After they drained their glasses, Julia went on, "I can't really believe this is happening, Longarm. Even if we're going to be together for a while, I want some proof that you're really here, and I don't want to wait for it. Come with me."

She took Longarm's hand and he followed without a word as she led him toward the back of the car. The stateroom they entered was dominated by a luxurious double bed that left barely enough space to pass. Julia's free hand had begun to free the fastening of her clinging robe when they passed through the door, and now she let the robe fall into shimmering folds around her feet. She was wearing nothing under it and Longarm looked with open admiration at her ivory body, its smoothness broken only by the dark pink tips of her generous upstanding breasts and the dark curls of her pubic brush. Stepping closer to him, she began unbuttoning his vest.

Longarm unbuckled his gun belt and let the weight of his holstered Colt carry it to the floor before levering out of his boots. Julia had his vest and shirt unbuttoned by now, and her fingers were busy with his belt buckle. He helped her as best he could to free his arms from the shirt and vest, and the warm smoothness of her skin as his hands brushed against her body now and then brought him to the beginning of an erection.

"Help me," Julia whispered as she fumbled with the buttons of Longarm's fly.

Their hands brushed and Julia's lips sought his again as they swayed, and their bared bodies brushed together while she tugged and pushed at his trousers and long johns until they dropped in a wrinkled heap to the floor. Freed of restraint now, his erection jutted upward. Julia's lips parted as the rhythm of her breathing increased. Her thrusting tongue met his as she pressed her hips closer to trap his swollen shaft between their bodies. Longarm closed his arms around her, lifted her from the floor and took the two short steps that brought them to the bed.

"Hurry!" she gasped, opening her thighs to place him. "I'm burning to feel . . ."

Her words trailed off into a small high-pitched cry of delight as Longarm drove into her. She lay supine, sounding out bubbling sighs of pleasure, then short gasps of delight as he continued his thrusts.

Now Longarm was as aroused as Julia. He drove furiously and she responded by bringing her hips up in a writhing roll each time he lunged. Bubbling gasps of ecstasy escaped her lips until Longarm slowed to a more deliberate pace. The gasps became slow trailing sighs that were barely audible until he ended his slowed penetrations with a lusty lunge and held himself pressed close to her quivering body.

They were both fully aroused by now. Longarm continued his rhythmic thrusting and Julia's body started to quiver without a moment of quiet interrupting the tremors, then he slowed the frantic tempo of his drives. He pressed himself close to her at the end of each lunge and waited for her shudders to subside before beginning to stroke again.

At last Julia whispered urgently, "Now, Longarm! I can't wait longer!"

Longarm resumed his quick drives. Julia was writhing now, her body tense and trembling. Gasps and small screams bubbled from her throat as she started a frenzy of

23

shuddering that ended in a few frantic twists when she cried out. Her body tensed in a rippling pulsing shudder. Longarm held himself pressed firmly against her as he joined in her quivering, and as he jetted, Julia uttered a final long sigh of ultimate pleasure before her body went limp and Longarm relaxed with her, pressing close.

Slowly their bodies grew still and they lay motionless. Then Julia whispered, "Don't go away, Longarm. I'm enjoying feeling you fill me."

"Not any more than I am," he replied. "We'll rest a while just like we are now. There ain't no need to hurry. We got a long, long ride ahead of us."

Chapter 3

"It doesn't seem like we've been together now for almost a week, Longarm," Julia remarked.

"No, it don't," he agreed. "I ain't even been trying to keep track of the time, myself, but it sure has slid past. And here we've been in San Francisco almost a full day and I ain't even checked up on my case yet."

"I'm flattered." Julia smiled. "I've always had the idea that your cases got your attention first."

"Like your business deals generally do?" Longarm asked.

"I suppose we are two of a kind, aren't we? Maybe that's why we get on so well together."

She and Longarm were sitting cuddled together on a sofa looking out the window of her suite on the top floor of the St. Francis Hotel. Below them the lights of San Francisco gleamed through a thin layer of fog that had begun settling early in the evening. In the middle distance the gleams were picked up in shimmering lines that stretched away from the shore until they were swallowed by the night-black waters of the bay.

"Maybe so. And I wouldn't swap the time we've had for anything."

"Neither would I," she said. "Especially the time we've spent in bed. Do you think there's a chance that we might be able to go back East together?"

"Just about none at all, Julia. From the way my chief talked when he was laying this job out for me, I might be here in California for quite a while."

"But not here in San Francisco?"

"Not likely."

Julia sighed and went on, "Perhaps it's just as well. I've got almost as much business in the southern part of the state as I have here. If you stayed, we'd probably spend all our time together and never get around to doing the things that brought us here."

"And tomorrow morning bright and early I got to report in at the Indian Bureau office. I'm sure Billy Vail's sent a telegram to the head man telling him when to expect me."

"Suppose I have dinner sent up to the suite here, then," she suggested. "And we'll just have to make the most of whatever time we have left together."

"I guess that'll have to be the way of it. But don't push the call-button for the waiter just yet. We've got to take advantage of our time to finish what we started when the train began slowing for the depot this morning."

"You want me to wait for you, mister?" the hackman asked as Longarm stepped out onto the sidewalk in front of the Federal Building late in the morning of the following day. He'd found the suite in the St. Francis boring after Julia had left to make a round of business visits, and decided that while she was otherwise occupied he'd be saving time later by getting his own affairs moving. The cabbie went on, "When you get as far down Market as Hyde it ain't like being right in the middle of town, where you can flag down a cab any time you happen to want one."

"I'll have to count on my luck being good, then," Longarm replied. "I might be here just a little while, or I might not get away for the rest of the day."

"Suit yourself, friend," the cabman said, though his voice was anything but friendly. He tucked away the money Longarm had handed him and flicked the reins over his nag's rump. "Just don't blame me if you get blisters on your feet from having to walk back."

Chuckling to himself at the independence shown by cabmen in virtually every large city he'd visited, Longarm found the office number of the Indian Bureau on the lobby directory and mounted the stairs to the second floor. He went through the door and stopped with a frown. The Indian Bureau office began with a narrow entry barely large enough to accommodate the desk and chair that were its sole furniture. A door in the frosted glass partition forming the wall of the tiny room bore the legend U.S. INDIAN BUREAU—PLEAS MCCARTHY, CHIEF AGENT, WEST COAST DISTRICT.

Stepping up to the door, Longarm tapped lightly on the door's opaque glass panel. There was a scuffle of feet on the floor beyond the door. It opened, and a slender blond man with a neatly trimmed Vandyke beard stared at him with a frown.

"Are you looking for somebody?" the man asked.

"If you're McCarthy, I've found the man I'm looking for. My name's Long, deputy marshal outa the Denver office. Are you the one that sent for me?"

"Marshal Long!" McCarthy exclaimed. He extended his hand and Longarm shook it. Then McCarthy went on, "Yes, of course I'm the one who sent for you—asked for you, really, through our Washington office, though I didn't

27

have much confidence that my request would be approved. In fact, if you come down to brass tacks, I'd just about given up on ever seeing you here, or anybody else I might ask for."

"That sounds to me like you've been having a little bit of a hard time." Longarm frowned.

"I have. And you're probably the only other man working for the United States government that I'd talk to about it. But why don't we step back into my office here, close the door and sit down? Then we can have a private talk without much chance of being interrupted."

McCarthy's office was uncarpeted and only a bit larger than the entry. It looked crowded even, though its furniture was limited to a modest sized desk, a tall wooden filing cabinet, and three straight-backed chairs. All five pieces bore the scars and stains of long hard use.

"I'll give you credit for one thing," Longarm remarked as he scanned the little room. "You sure ain't like them Indian Bureau men back in the Nation, with their big fancy offices and high-priced furnishings."

"To say nothing of graft from suppliers and stealing from bureau appropriations," McCarthy added bitterly. He went around the desk and gestured for Longarm to take the chair across from him as he went on, "And when an agent like myself doesn't join the thieves' ring, they pull strings to get me stationed in places like San Francisco, where there's no activity to speak of. They don't want to put in any time in a city like this, where there's no chance for graft."

"I thought all that was finished when I helped bust up that ring of thieves that had just about taken over the bureau back in the Indian Nation," Longarm said with a frown.

"I know there's still some grafting going on," McCarthy assured him. "And some stealing, too. But it's not on as big a scale and not as open, and it's pretty well confined to the Indian Nation and to Washington."

"How about out here in California?" Longarm asked. "Ain't that why you asked the Justice Department to send me here?"

McCarthy shook his head. "No. It's something that might get even more serious unless you can stop it."

"You mean your Indian police can't handle it?"

"We don't have the force here in California like we do back in the Nation, Marshal Long. All I've got in this office is one part-time helper. And even if I had a half dozen men, I'm not sure they'd be able to handle the trouble that's coming to a head here on the West Coast. It could be worse than the little war they had about ten years ago, up in the Modoc County lava beds."

"Well, now," Longarm said, "that's something I didn't know about. Maybe you better tell me."

"It started in Yreka, that's just south of the Oregon line and not too far from where you'll be going. The Modoc tribe had a headman called Captain Jack—some say he was a half-breed, but I don't guess much of anybody knows the truth. To cut the story as short as possible, the Modocs fought our boys in blue for damn near a year. They never did come close to winning, but they put up some good fights."

"I don't guess I need to guess the end," Longarm said when McCarthy stopped for breath. "The army caught up with this Captain Jack and shot him."

"Hanged him and his main men," McCarthy emended. "But it cost a lost of money, and from what I've heard there's still bad feelings about it up there. The brass in the Indian Bureau in Washington don't want to see it happen again."

"So that's what I got in front of me," Longarm said, shaking his head. "When Billy Vail told me I was going to get sent out here on detached duty in your outfit, I just figured this case here'd be pretty much like that one back in the Indian Nation."

"We've got different kinds of Indians out here, Marshal Long," McCarthy explained. "Remember, the Spaniards began settling here on the West Coast something like a hundred years before the pilgrims came ashore at Plymouth Rock."

"I guess if I ever heard about that, I've forgotten it," Longarm confessed.

"So has almost everybody else," the Indian agent replied. "But those early settlers started taming the redskins along the coast way back then. Between the Spanish settlers coming up from Mexico and the Russians from the north—"

"Wait a minute!" Longarm exclaimed. "How in tunket do the Russians come into it?"

"Why, they started coming south from Alaska," McCarthy explained. "Built themselves a fort a hundred miles or so north of the bay here. They logged and took sea otter furs and sealskins for, well, a good forty or fifty years, until enough of our people got here during the Gold Rush to send 'em home."

"Maybe I didn't get what you was saying just right," Longarm said. "Especially when you started talking about the redskins a minute ago. You'd have to be concerned with Indians of some sort, or why else would the Indian Bureau have this office here?"

"That's the official reason," the Indian agent answered. "If you want to know the truth, most of the time my jobs are just about as useful as tits on a bull. The fact of the matter, Marshal, is that if you gathered up all the Indians from all the tribes in northern California, you'd find there just aren't as many as you may have imagined."

"Then why'd I get sent all the way out here? My orders

are to help you tame down a bunch of hostiles."

"Because there's a real possibility that those tame Indians we're talking about might turn into hostiles, like the Modocs, this time against the loggers."

"But from what you just said, there ain't enough of 'em to kick up all that much of a fuss."

"If you put all the tribes together, they could cause some trouble," McCarthy assured him.

"How many tribes have you got to deal with?"

"Let's see. There's the Tolowas and the Yuroks, Wiyots, Klamaths and Wintus. Then there's the Patwins and the Wishoks and the Karoks and Chimarikos and Yukis," McCarthy went on. "And the Sinkyones and Pomos and Hoopas." He paused for a moment, then said, "I don't think I've missed any of them."

"Well, that's a baker's dozen right there," Longarm said. "How big a group are we talking about when you put 'em all together?"

"Not as big as it might sound, Marshal Long. There's not more than thirty or forty Indians in any one of the biggest tribes. The little ones—well, I'd say maybe ten or a dozen in the two or three smallest."

"That ain't enough to make a lot of war parties out of," Longarm said. "I'd imagine the loggers'd have 'em outnumbered by a good bit."

"Of course they would! And none of the tribes I've named are fighters. But that doesn't stop the loggers from wanting to get rid of them. You see, almost all the tribes, even the ones that don't add up to more than ten or a dozen people, have some kind of claim on a good chunk or two of prime timberland."

"Which the loggers want, I'd imagine," Longarm added.

"And they don't have any scruples about stealing, or killing a few Indians to get their hands on it. Why, just a

31

little while back, there was a real bad fracas up at Humboldt Bay. A bunch of loggers killed maybe fifteen or twenty of one of the tribes that were living peacefully on an island in the bay."

"What started the killing?"

"Nothing that I've been able to find out, and the sheriff up in Humboldt is just as puzzled as I am. He said the Indians hadn't been doing anything out of the ordinary. And they didn't put up a fight, 'cause the only weapons they had were two or three old flintlocks. The loggers just went out one night and started shooting."

"And you haven't heard about any more dust-ups since then?"

McCarthy shook his head. "No. But there could've been some that I didn't hear about. News is slow getting here from that stretch of country up the coast."

"What's wrong with the telegraph?"

"There isn't any north of the city here. There's no railroad, nor even a wagon road that's easy to travel over. If you want to go up there fast, you take a boat. If you don't mind riding upgrade over rough country, you can go horseback. And usually any news of what's happening up there in the north doesn't trickle down here to San Francisco for a month or more."

"Well, redskins is redskins in my book," Longarm said. "I got a few Indian friends back in the Nation, but for the most part I go my way and let them go theirs. From what you've said, the Indians don't seem to be giving anybody any trouble."

"They haven't started anything yet," McCarthy admitted. "They haven't even tried to avenge those killings up at Humboldt Bay. But I'm bothered about some whispers I've heard."

"Such as what?"

"That trouble's going to start between them and the loggers. It seems the streams are getting so cluttered up with slash from logging that the Indians aren't able to fish. And they depend on fishing for most of their food."

"If you don't mind me saying so," he told McCarthy, "I'm not sure what you had me sent out here for. Looks to me like you're just handing me a job that's up to you to do."

"There's a chance I might agree with you if Indians were all that's involved," McCarthy replied. "But loggers are another matter. They aren't obliged to listen to me and there's not a sheriff up in the redwood country who'll pay any attention when I try to get them to make the loggers go easy on the rivers."

"Well, that don't seem—" Longarm stopped when the sound of the outer door opening reached their ears.

"Excuse me, Marshal Long," McCarthy said. "I'll have to go see who it is that's just come in."

Longarm nodded as the Indian agent rose from his chair and went out to the outer office. He'd left the door ajar a crack and Longarm heard him ask, "What can I do for you?"

McCarthy's question was answered by a shot. The explosion echoed and reechoed through the inner office.

Longarm started toward the door. He drew his Colt as he stepped around the end of the desk that crowded the little room. He moved as fast as possible in the small crowded area, but before he could open the connecting door he heard the door to the hall slam shut and a flurry of thunking boot heels dying away.

A glance was all he needed to tell him that he could do nothing for the Indian agent. McCarthy lay motionless, his crumpled corpse sprawled facedown on the floor. A trickle of bright blood ran from the gaping exit wound of a bullet that had torn away most of the back of his skull.

Longarm did not waste time trying to examine the dead

man's body. He burst through the door into the hall. It was empty and every door along its length was closed.

Heading for the stairway, Longarm took the steps to the ground floor two at a time. He looked along the street in both directions, but saw no one among the few pedestrians who seemed to be hurrying to escape from the scene of a crime. He hailed the nearest passerby.

"Where'll I find a policeman?" he asked the man.

"If you'll just step up to the corner of Market Street, I'd imagine you'll find one not too far away."

Longarm took out his wallet and flipped it open to show his badge. "Deputy United States marshal," he said. "Name is Custis Long. If it's all that easy to find a policeman, I'll just deputize you to find one for me. There's been a murder in this building here. I got to stay till a policeman can come take charge, so if you'll go find me one, I'll be much obliged."

"Always ready to help the law, Marshal. There ought to be one pretty close by, probably up Market Street. I'll see if I can find him for you."

"Tell him I'll be up in the Indian Bureau office," Longarm called as the man started away. "It's on the second floor!"

He saw the man turn and wave in acknowledgment, then went back inside and returned to the Indian Bureau office. For a moment Longarm stood motionless, looking at McCarthy's sprawled body. He was sure there was nothing he could learn from the corpse, but took time to make a cursory exploration of the dead agent's pockets. He found only a small amount of money, a handkerchief and a ring holding three or four keys. After he returned them to the dead man's pockets, he stepped across the corpse and returned to the inner office.

There was nothing except a few sheets of Indian Bureau letterhead in the drawers of the desk, but the tall filing cabinet was stuffed with manila folders. Each of them bore the name of one of the Indian tribes that McCarthy had mentioned during the brief conversation between him and Longarm. While a few of the folders contained only a few sheets of paper, most of them were stuffed.

Longarm stood motionless for a few moments looking at the names on the file tabs. He was still studying them when the doorknob of the hall door rattled and he turned. Through the open door to the small room where McCarthy's body lay, Longarm saw a blue-uniformed policeman.

"Anybody here?" the officer called.

"I've been waiting for you," Longarm replied. As he stepped to the door connecting the two rooms he took his wallet from his pocket and extended it for the policeman to see.

"Well," the officer said, "federal marshal, eh? I don't recall seeing you before."

"It ain't likely you have, seeing as how I work out of the Denver office," Longarm told the man.

"Oh, I ain't doubting you're who this badge says you are, Marshal Long," the policeman said hurriedly. "But if you ain't, the gumshoe boys will find out right quick when they get here."

"I take it the gumshoe boys are your detective squad?"

"Yep. I punched 'em up at my call box to headquarters when some fellow told me there'd been a killing here. They'll show up in a few minutes. I don't guess you mind waiting."

"Not a bit. Except there's not much of anything I can tell your men, even though I was sitting across the desk from McCarthy just a minute or two before he was shot."

"And you didn't see who fired the shot?"

"I was sitting with my back to the door. Whoever it was just yanked the door open, waited for McCarthy, shot, then

35

slammed the door and ran. I didn't glimpse hair nor hide of 'em."

"Well, save your story for the gumshoes, Marshal Long. I won't be on the case, and there's no use in you having to repeat it. They'll want you to go over things two or three times. Just have a seat and wait. They oughta show up any minute now."

Leaning back in the chair, Longarm slid a cigar from his vest pocket and flicked a match into life. The Indian Bureau office was quiet now after the detectives had finished their work and the mortuary wagon had removed McCarthy's body.

Looking at the bulging manila folder on the desk, Longarm sighed at the prospect of plowing through it as well as the others in the file cabinet. He'd taken the folder from the filing cabinet after the detective squad and the mortuary people had left.

"Whoever it was that killed that poor devil must've had a good reason for taking the risk in broad open daylight," Longarm said in the silence of the cramped little office. "And if it wasn't somebody McCarthy had fell out with over a woman or something, there might be answers in them files. So you might as well start digging, old son. You've found out what this job is all about, and the quicker you get started on it, the quicker you'll close your case."

Clamping the cigar in his strong teeth, Longarm opened the file folder and began scanning through the pages.

Chapter 4

Longarm laid aside the last page of the thick sheaf of papers he'd been going through and looked up at the Regulator clock on the office wall. He saw with surprise that its hands stood only a few minutes away from midnight. He was aware that his eyes were smarting from the strain of scanning through the mass of papers he'd taken from the murdered Indian agent's files, and at the same time his stomach was sending him urgent signals that it was empty.

"Damned if you ain't got the kind of hunger a starved prairie wolf gets after a big snowstorm, old son!" Longarm exclaimed. "And it's a sure bet that Julia's wondering what in tunket's happened to keep you from showing up. You better hump outa here in a hurry and get back to the hotel before she gets real upset!"

Blowing out the kerosene lamp on the desk, Longarm locked the office door and clattered down the stairs two steps at a time. At some point during the hours he'd been working, San Francisco's traditional evening fog had settled in. He looked in vain along the deserted street toward the nimbus of lights that glowed from Market Street, hoping he'd see a hackney cab, but in his limited field of vision there was neither a pedestrian nor a vehicle of any sort visible.

His boot heels thunking on the uneven bricks of the sidewalk, he started toward the lights. Once in the Market Street commercial district he had no trouble hailing a cab, and within a few minutes was alighting in the wide porte cochere of the St. Francis Hotel. A slow elevator ride later, he knocked at the door of Julia's suite.

"What on earth happened to you, Longarm?" Julia asked as she opened the door. She stepped into his waiting arms and tilted her head back to meet his lips. After they'd broken their embrace, she went on, "I didn't begin to be concerned until a couple of hours after dinnertime, and then I had no idea what to think."

"I just played the fool," Longarm admitted, following her into the parlor of the suite that was their temporary haven. "But a lot of things happened. Me and the Indian agent were right in the middle of our confab when somebody came into his office and gunned him down."

"You were in a gunfight?" Julia exclaimed.

"I didn't even see the killer, let alone have a chance to stop him. McCarthy was in another room when he got shot and whoever did it was gone before I could get to where the shooting was. I never even set eyes on him. I had to call in the San Francisco police, and after they got through with their job I began going through McCarthy's papers to see if I could find out who might've wanted to kill him. I sorta let the time slip past, that's why I'm so late getting back here."

"You must be starved then!"

"Well, I ain't all that bad off, but don't take that to

mean I'd say no to a bite of something. I guess you've already had your supper?"

"I have and I haven't. You know how I hate to eat alone, Longarm. When you didn't come in after I'd waited a while, I ordered a chafing-dish supper sent up here for us."

"I sure hope it ain't some kind of hashed-up meat that's drowned in a slather of flour gravy."

"Give me credit for knowing you well enough not to make that mistake," Julia said, smiling. "I know how you are about leftovers. I got some slices of veal in a good sauce, and I've left the chafing-dish burner on, so the food's still hot and ready to eat."

"Well, now, that sounds tasty enough."

"It is. When you still weren't back and I began to feel really hungry, I ate a few bites to tide me over. But by this time I'm hungry again, so we'll have our real dinner together."

"Now, that's the best news yet," Longarm said. "And I don't even need a shot of Tom Moore to rouse my appetite. Let's just go right on in and sit down."

After the first bites of the tender veal slices had taken the edge off their appetites, Longarm began giving Julia a condensed account of his visit to the Indian Bureau office and how it had culminated with the murder of Pleas McCarthy.

"So you see why I couldn't leave right away," he concluded. "I had to stay there at the Indian Bureau and go through them papers page by page so I'd get some idea of where I'd have to be going and maybe get an idea about somebody who'd have a grudge against McCarthy."

"And did you find anything?"

"If it's evidence you're asking about, there wasn't a smithereen. Of course, with him dead, whoever takes his place might not want to do what McCarthy had figured to."

"You'll know the answer to that pretty soon, I'm sure," Julia assured him. "In the meantime, let's just enjoy the time we have left here. In three or four days my business in San Francisco will be finished and I'm going to have to leave and go to Los Angeles."

Longarm had known from the beginning of their trip that he and Julia could not be together very long. He wasted no words in protest, but nodded and replied, "That's about how long it's going to take to get things all straightened out at the Indian Bureau, naming a new chief and all. And maybe by then the city police will have come up with a lead on whoever it was that killed Pleas McCarthy."

"From what you've told me, just about every logger along the north coast of California could qualify for wanting to get rid of your Mr. McCarthy," Julia said thoughtfully. "And from what I've seen of them on the timber stands there are plenty who wouldn't have any hesitation at all about pulling the trigger. There are a lot of very tough men up in the redwoods."

Longarm's eyes opened wider as he asked, "You know that country north from here along the coast?"

"Not well," she admitted. "But I spent something like six months traveling back and forth along it with my father, looking at different logging stands, just before he died."

"And you didn't mention it once these past few days while we've been together!"

"We had other things to keep us busy, if you remember," Julia teased. "And I don't remember that you ever told me exactly where your case was taking you."

Now Longarm's smile matched Julia's. After a moment he went on, "I don't guess you've been there lately?"

Julia shook her head. "No. After Father's death I didn't have any interest in adding something new to all the businesses that I'd inherited from him, even after learning how much money can be made in it."

"You're bound to remember a lot of what you saw up there, though," Longarm suggested.

"Of course. I'm sure there've been changes since I was there last, but the land itself can't have changed all that much."

For a moment Longarm sat thoughtfully silent, then he said slowly, "Up till now, we've been real careful not to nose into each other's business affairs, Julia. And I don't want that to change, because the way we've been doing things worked out real fine. But I need to find out about that redwood country from somebody I can trust. Not people's names or anything about 'em, but just the lay of the land. It's one place I'm not too familiar with."

"You're going up there, of course," Julia offered. She was silent for a moment, then went on, "Well, it's different from any other place in the world I've ever been. But I don't see why I shouldn't tell you what I remember about the land itself, without pointing any fingers at the people."

"I've found out that people are pretty much the same wherever you run into 'em," Longarm replied. "There's good ones and bad ones and ones you remember and ones you forget. But I'd sure like to know something about that country up there, at least enough to keep me from making a lot of fool mistakes."

"When Father and I were in the redwood country most of the coast wasn't even settled," Julia pointed out. She was obviously searching her memory for details only half remembered.

Before she could continue, Longarm said, "I don't need too much of the fine points, Julia. Just a little bit about the towns and how to get around."

"I remember the magnificent redwood trees better than I

do anything else," Julia told him thoughtfully. "You've got to see them to believe them."

"Trees don't concern me much," Longarm said. "Tell me about the towns."

"There were only two or three real towns when I was there," she went on. "Oh, there were places close to the river mouths where a few little shanties were left after the loggers moved out of one of their camps."

"I don't suppose you noticed the Indians, if there were any around?"

"I'm sure I must've seen some, but I can't recall anything about them. And I met the bosses of the logging camps, but all I noticed about the loggers was that they had to work hard. From daybreak to dark. There weren't any distractions in the logging camps."

"From the way you talk, I don't guess things have changed much," Longarm decided. "Especially if there's not anything up along that north coast but a lot of trees."

"Trees and rivers," she agreed. "And very few roads."

"I guess boats carry folks up the rivers?"

Julia shook her head. "The rivers up there are too wild for boats."

"What about the roads?"

"Except for the one that runs along the coast there aren't any to speak of. Mostly old logging roads that were made by ox teams and mule teams. Where there aren't any rivers to float the logs to the coast, the loggers use ox teams and mule teams to drag the logs to the ocean."

"You mean they'd float the logs all the way down here to San Francisco?"

"Oh, no. There are three or four sawmills on Humboldt Bay, and they cut the trees into boards. Ships can put into the bay to load and unload. But it's the only really good harbor north of the Golden Gate. The only two towns that amount to anything are on the bay, Eureka and Arcata."

"I reckon the army's got some forts along the way, though, and north of there, too. I sorta depend on getting cavalry remount horses when I'm working a case away from Denver."

Again Julia shook her head. "The army moved out of all the forts they'd built along the coast when the war started, and never did move back. There were some buildings left of the fort that was on Humboldt Bay, but the others were gone."

"You said you didn't have much to do with the Indians?"

"I'm sure I saw some Indians, but that was all. The loggers didn't seem to have much use for them then, and I don't suppose that's changed much."

"It ain't changed a bit. I found that out reading all them reports in the Indian Bureau files," Longarm confirmed. "But if I'm going up there anyway, after all that's happened, I'll just do the best I can to get everything settled down and peaceful, then I can get back to Denver where I feel more at home."

Longarm did not feel at all at home as he looked across the bow of the side-wheel steamship that was standing off the coast at the mouth of the narrow inlet leading into Humboldt Bay. He was still in low spirits, though three days had passed since he and Julia had said their good-byes. They had assured each other that they'd be able to get together again soon, though both of them knew that such a promise was impossible to keep.

Since boarding the *Ocean Gem*, a coastal passenger ship that plied the Pacific from Los Angeles to Vancouver, Longarm had felt his usual discomfort at being anywhere except on solid land. He'd stayed in his cramped cabin most of the time, feeling a bit uneasy in spite of the fact that the sea had been calm during the entire voyage.

Each time he'd stepped out on deck and looked at the white-tipped waves that surrounded the small coastal vessel, he'd been able to turn his eyes to the shoreline and get the assurance that solid land was not far away. Now, with the *Ocean Gem*'s big paddle wheels barely turning, he turned his attention to the waves ahead as they curled and foamed when they broke against the rugged shoreline, which rose on both sides of what seemed to him to be the very narrow gap through which the vessel must pass to enter the bay.

"Old son," he muttered, "if you'd had any sense you'd just have picked out a good horse from a livery stable in San Francisco and rode it up here like anybody with brains would've. Getting this big ship through that little gap is gonna be a lot tougher than threading a needle without wetting down the end of the thread."

Sunset was still more than an hour away. The bright glow of the declining sun bathed the coastline and showed every towering tree that stood beyond the glowing brown rocks. For each tree there seemed to be two stumps, which stood like massive brown stubby fangs that filled the area between the still-growing trees and the wide expanse of rocky beach that stretched to the roiled surface of the Pacific.

Longarm studied the forbidding expanse of coastline for a moment before returning his attention to the gap. Since reaching its present position in midafternoon the ship had been cruising slowly back and forth in front of the break in the shoreline where the waters of the bay merged with those of the ocean in a roiling line of frothy white.

When Longarm had asked one of the *Ocean Gem*'s officers why the vessel wasn't sailing right on into the bay, the man's reply had done nothing to ease his mind.

"Except for a half hour or so at high tide, the water's not deep enough for us to get over the sandbar across the mouth of the bay," the officer had told him. "We've got to wait until the tide turns before we try to sail over it."

"When does all that happen?"

"About an hour before sundown today. I suppose you know the tides rise and fall twice a day?"

"That's about all I do know. I ain't spent much time around the seacoast."

"Well, you don't really have anything to worry about. We do this every trip. I've been on the *Gem* for nearly a year now and we've only been hung up in the gap four or five times."

"Hung up? You mean on the bottom?"

"Of course. But don't waste your time fretting, mister. Only a few of the bigger freighters have to worry about getting stranded on the harbor bar, and generally it only happens when they're carrying too much cargo. Now, on this trip we're sailing light, so we'll make it today."

"And how long did you say that water in the gap stays deep enough to float the ship?"

"Oh, usually about half an hour or so. Time enough for us to make a second run at it if we don't get across on the first try. Like I said, you don't have a thing to worry about."

Touching his cap, the officer had strolled away. Long-arm watched him disappear into the wheelhouse before turning his attention back to the shore. The distant tinkle of a signal bell reached his ears and the pulsing of the ship's engines, which had been a slow regular beat, increased appreciably.

Longarm was watching the shoreline now, concentrating his attention on the expanse of open water that stretched between the two points of land. He was not aware at first that the vessel's big side-wheel paddles were moving faster until the spray they'd begun to raise began escaping from the wheel housings and drops of water splashed onto his back.

He turned to look and saw the great wheels churning the sea to froth as the vessel quickly picked up speed. Though he'd taken his eyes off the shoreline for only a moment, when Longarm swiveled his head to face the bow again he dodged involuntarily. The low wall of green saplings and vines that grew on the rocky spits seemed to be rushing toward him while the ship seemed to stand still.

Scattered drops of spraying water began hitting Longarm's face. He ducked in reflex action when the first wet spatters struck his face, then began looking for the source of the dripping shower. The origin of the spray was not hard to find. The smaller drops were the sprays still escaping around the arched wheel housings, and the big splashing blobs hitting his face were being thrown up from the enlarging bow wave.

In spite of the spattering he was receiving, Longarm stood his ground. Only a few dozen yards lay between the ship's bow and the gap. Suddenly the rocky rising spits of land on each side seemed close enough to touch. The ship's bow rose suddenly, but Longarm was accustomed to keeping his balance on a bucking horse and instinctively he did the right thing by relaxing his knees to absorb the shock.

He could see the surface roiling ahead where the inrushing tide collided with the water of the bay. The force of the current as the ocean's water rose seemed to lift the ship's deck, and in spite of his widespread feet and braced legs Longarm teetered at the sudden shock and almost fell. He kept his balance, however, but he could feel the deck under his feet continue to rise and tightened his grip on the rail.

Suddenly an ominous scraping sound rose above the susurrus of the disturbed water and the *Ocean Gem* shuddered for a moment. Then it plunged forward again, the boards of the deck tilting under Longarm's feet. The unexpected change in his footing sent him sliding into the ship's rail, and he found himself looking almost straight down at the ocean's roiled surface.

A huge oval-topped wave was climbing the ship's prow. It seemed to be rising up the vessel's sides toward the deck, and Longarm stepped back involuntarily. Just as he released his grip on the rail to leap backward the ship shuddered again, the bow wave diminished as suddenly as it had formed, and the vibrations of the engines, which had been keeping the deck in a constant quiver, subsided rapidly.

Turning to look back, Longarm was surprised to see that the vessel had cut through the massive hump of water. Its ripples were now behind him. The gap that the ship had just passed through seemed to be shrinking in size as it receded rapidly. The shuddering of the deck under his feet diminished to mild vibrations. Belatedly Longarm realized that there were no drops of water being flung back now by the bow wave. He stepped to the rail to glance down at the water's surface and saw that it was almost calm, though still dotted with a number of gentle humps.

When he raised his eyes to squint at the reddening sun, he was surprised to see that its bottom was almost at the horizon's rim. Blinking, he turned to look ahead. Humboldt Bay was much larger than he'd expected it to be. He could not see land at its southern rim, and to the north the water bulged in a huge placid and almost circular expanse.

Directly ahead the buildings of a small town stretched along the level expanse of shoreline, and between the small trees that rose between the stumps of felled giants on the upslope beyond there were scattered houses. As his eyes moved along the shoreline he saw other large buildings clustered near the edge of the bay in several places. Their size and the faint distant screech of sawblades that broke

47

the air now and then enabled him to identify them as mills. Between the mills and the houses there were broad stretches of stump-filled land, and a few more houses were scattered in cut-over areas beyond the mills.

Engrossed in his study of the bayshore, Longarm turned with a start when a man behind him said, "Coming into the bay wasn't as rough as you thought it'd be, was it?" It was the ship's officer, to whom he'd been talking earlier. Before he could reply to the man's question, the officer went on, "You'll have plenty of time to go ashore here and look around. We can't leave until the next tide turn, and that'll be about four o'clock tomorrow morning."

"Thanks for the tip, but this is as far as I got a ticket to go anyhow," Longarm replied. "I got to admit I'm sorta surprised. From what I heard in San Francisco, I didn't figure Eureka was such a good-sized place."

"It's not. You're really looking at two towns," the man said. "We'll be putting in at the wharf in Eureka, that's the one just ahead. The little settlement to the north is Arcata."

"I don't imagine I'll have trouble in one or the other finding a livery stable where I can rent me a horse?"

"No trouble at all. And there are plenty of rooming houses where you can get a bed for the night. But if you don't mind a bit of advice, keep your eyes open and your mouth shut if you go into a saloon. The loggers up here don't take very kindly to strangers and they're ready to fight at the drop of a hat."

"I'll keep it in mind," Longarm said. "And thanks for the tip." He looked ahead at the shoreline, where people were beginning to assemble on a wharf that extended into the bay. "I guess I better get my stuff outa my cabin. Looks like we're just about to the pier, and all of a sudden I got a real hankering to get my feet planted on solid land again."

Chapter 5

Darkness was shrouding the street as Longarm came out of the rooming house where he'd found accommodations for the night. During the past hour he'd been busy at a string of chores that needed to be done after disembarking from the *Ocean Gem*. Every outer garment he'd taken off—his trousers, coat and vest—was stiff with streaks of gleaming white dried salt from the sprays that had swept across him while he was standing on the ship's deck during its passage over the bar on entering the mouth of Humboldt Bay.

After dropping his saddlebags and rifle and trying the bed in the cramped little room, he'd begun his chores by sponging his long brown coat and trousers to remove the crusted salt. While his outer clothing dried, he'd had his bath and shaved in the tiny cubicle of a bathroom at the end of the hall. Feeling better in a fresh shirt and his now-presentable trousers and coat, he was more than ready to respond to the urgent signals for food that his stomach had been sending out for the past quarter of an hour.

Looking along the unpaved street, Longarm saw the un-mistakable glare of acetylene lights ahead. The brilliant bluish hue of the new kind of illumination could not be mistaken for any other kind of light. Surprised and curious, Longarm started toward the bright spot. He covered two of the short city blocks before reaching his goal. Stopping at the corner, he glanced to his right, then to his left.

He saw no one on the street. Along it for a block in both directions acetylene lights dangled in front of signs placed on the gables of the low-roofed buildings that lined the street. All the signs had one thing in common. The first line or two of each one bore a fanciful name, and always in oversized letters the bottom line read BAR or SALOON.

For a few moments Longarm stood scanning the signs. There was LOGGER'S REST, REDWOOD, TALL TREE, LONE TREE, BIG TREES, GREEN TREE, HIGH TIMBER, SAWYER'S, and a few more that in spite of the brilliant lights were too far away or had letters too small for him to read.

"Well, old son," Longarm told himself as he turned and started down the street of saloons, "there never was a place yet where the barkeeps don't know more'n the police chief about what's going on in a town and all around it. All you got to do is try out these saloons until you find a barkeep that's got a flap jaw, and there's sure plenty of 'em here for you to work on. There's bound to be one where you can sip a tot of Maryland rye and ask a few questions about where places are and what's going on in 'em."

In contrast to the ease with which he'd found Eureka's saloon row, Longarm had more trouble than he'd antici-pated in discovering which of the establishments, if any, kept Maryland rye on their backbar.

Starting at the corner, he pushed in turn through the batwings of the Logger's Rest, the Tall Tree, the Big Trees and the High Timber saloons and asked for his favorite whiskey. In the first three the aproned barkeeps glanced at him with sour faces and shook their heads. In the fourth, the barkeep did not reply in so many words, but laughed in a burst of loud guffawing and suggested that he perform a sexual feat that would have been anatomically impossible.

More than a little irked, his normally level temper stirred by the rudeness of the barkeepers, Longarm moved on to the Green Tree Saloon and repeated his order. In contrast to the busy drinking spots he'd just visited, the Green Tree was deserted except for the white-aproned barkeep and a single patron, who'd quite obviously had several drinks too many, for he was sprawled in a chair, his head and chest resting on a table, his arms outstretched on either side.

By now Longarm had decided there was little chance that he'd find his favorite liquor at any of the saloons, but this time he was pleasantly surprised to discover that he'd hit pay dirt at last. When he ordered Tom Moore Maryland rye the barkeep did not blink an eye, but nodded and turned to the bottle-lined shelves of the backbar.

He selected an almost empty bottle and wiped away its film of dust on his apron before placing the bottle and a shot glass on the bar's scarred unpolished wood. Digging into his pocket, Longarm slid a silver cartwheel across to the barkeep and filled the glass. When he replaced the bottle on the bar he noticed how little remained in it.

"I'd about given up finding any real whiskey in this town," he said. "I looked all along the street before I stepped in here, but every saloon I tried didn't have anything but that damn sweet bourbon. I sure didn't look to find a bottle of Tom Moore in a place—"

The barkeep broke in to finish his remark, saying, "In a place as run down as this." He nodded. "Well, I can't say I blame you, but I just bought out the fellow that let it get in such bad shape. This is the first night I've been open. I'll be fixing things up in here soon as I can, but it's going to take a little while."

Longarm had already tossed off the tot of rye while the man was talking. He set his glass down and pushed it closer to the bottle. "I could stand another swallow or so, but this bottle's so close to being empty as to make no never-mind."

"If I remember rightly, there's a full one in the storage room. It's right behind the bar," the bar owner told him. "You have what's left in that one—on the house, there ain't enough in it to charge you for—and I'll go bring in that fresh one from out back."

Picking up the bottle, Longarm started to empty it into his glass as the barkeep turned and started toward a door set into the wall behind the bar. He moved slowly and stiffly, and just before he reached the door and disappeared Longarm saw for the first time that his left knee rested in the crotch of a peg leg. Shaking his head in sympathy, he finished pouring the dregs of the whiskey into his glass.

Before he reached for his drink, Longarm began fumbling in his vest pocket for a cigar. He was taking the stogie out of his pocket when a thud of footfalls on the floor behind him reached his ears. He turned quickly, but not quickly enough to dodge the rush of the man he'd taken to be a sleeping drunk. The stranger had already covered most of the distance from the table where he'd been sprawled. His right hand was raised, and in it he held a long bulging leather slungshot.

Longarm was still poised in his half turn, his right side pressed to the bar, the overhanging edge of the scarred mahogany forming a barrier between his hand and his holstered Colt. Before he could lean forward and get a firm grip on the revolver's butt, his assailant completed the swing with his bulging blackjack. Longarm's hat absorbed some of the blow's impact, but the heavy slungshot still landed with enough force to stun him.

Toppling forward, Longarm began sagging to the floor, but the reflexes that had served him so well in so many desperate moments had been honed until his moves were almost instinctive. His attacker was turning now and starting to lift the blackjack for a second blow. Though only half conscious, Longarm managed to get his hand on his Colt's butt. He whipped it from its holster and let off a snapshot as he crumpled to the floor.

Although he was fighting to keep his senses and straining to hold his drooping eyelids open, Longarm was aware that the slug from his Colt had gone home. The man who'd attacked him was jackknifing backward now. His head was hunched forward, his shoulders drooping, his arms limp. The slungshot was slowly sliding from his hand.

Shaking his head, trying to clear his mind after the blow that had half stunned him, Longarm reached as high as he could and got a hand on the rounded edge of the bar. Slowly, he began to pull himself up, but the heavy blow he'd taken was still having its effect on his control of his muscles. His grip lacked the firmness to get a solid grasp on the rounded edge of the bar and he was still fighting to lock his fingers in place when the thunking of the barkeep's wooden leg reached his ears. The brokenly punctuated footsteps grew louder as the saloon keeper rounded the end of the bar and made his way to Longarm's side.

"Here," he said, "this'll bring you around quicker than anything else."

As he spoke the barkeep was twisting the cork out of the bottle of Tom Moore that was still in his hand. He bent forward and passed the bottle to Longarm, who managed to hold on to it and raise the neck to his lips. He let a sip of the sharp biting rye trickle down his throat, and though his shoulders and torso were still swaying, the liquor warming his throat and the sharp pungent fumes passing through his nostrils began to revive him. Lifting his head, he glanced at the sprawled body of the man who'd attacked him, then raised his eyes to look up at the saloon's proprietor.

"You got any idea who that fellow is, and why he took a notion to jump me?" he asked.

Shaking his head, the saloon man replied, "I never saw him before that I know of. He came in about a half hour ago, and he sure didn't act like he'd put away too much. He took a bottle over to that table where he was sitting when you come in, and I didn't pay all that much attention to him. Then all of a sudden he sagged across the table, and when I tried to rouse him, I'd've sworn he'd just passed out drunk."

"He sure didn't act drunk when he jumped me," Longarm said as he scrambled to his feet and set the bottle of Tom Moore on the bar. By this time he'd thrown off the effects of the stunning blow and both his mind and his muscles were functioning normally again. "And that barroom trick he tried to pull on me is so old it's got a full set of whiskers on it. Little petty crooks like him have been using it as long as I can remember."

"I guess I'm too green in the saloon business to've learned about it," the barkeep said ruefully. "Lumberjacking's about all I've ever worked at. But with my leg gone—" He indicated his wooden leg with a rueful gesture and shook his head. "And this is sure one hell of a way to start out as a saloon keeper. Having a shooting scrape in here and a dead man to show for it is going to give this place a bad name before I even get started."

"Now, hold on a minute!" Longarm told him quickly. "I'm the one that did the shooting, and that fellow laying there had already proved he was up to no good."

"You think you can make the sheriff here believe that?"

"I don't imagine that'll be too big of a job," Longarm

replied. He took out the wallet containing his badge and credentials and flipped it open to show the barkeep. "My name's Long, Custis Long. U.S. marshal, like it says on the badge. I generally work outa the Denver office, but on this case I'm reporting to the Indian Bureau in San Francisco. I was aiming to go introduce myself to the sheriff here, because I just might have to look to him to give me a hand with this case I'm on."

A sigh of relief escaped the bar owner's lips. Extending his hand he said, "My name's Charley Hudson, Marshal Long. And I don't mind telling you, I feel one hell of a lot better than I did a few minutes ago."

"Just leave this business for me to clean up," Longarm went on as the two men shook hands. "Don't move that fellow's body till I go get the sheriff and bring him back here. If he's anything like a reasonable man, you won't have one thing to worry about."

"You'll find the sheriff's office about six squares down the street and another four or five to the right," Hudson told him. "His name's Sam Carter, and that's all I know about him. I never have met him, myself."

"I'll run him down, or one of his men, anyhow," Longarm promised. "You just sit tight."

Longarm took his usual long strides as he followed Hudson's directions after leaving the saloon. Even from a distance he could spot the yellow brick building that housed the county's offices. At that hour of the night only one set of windows was lighted and he headed toward them. A sign, HUMBOLDT COUNTY SHERIFF'S OFFICE, dangled above the door of the lighted rooms.

Longarm felt at home the minute he stepped inside. At a counter that stretched the width of the narrow room a man wearing a law officer's star stood copying entries from a massive book onto some sort of printed forms. A second man lounged in a barrel chair, his feet propped up on the desk beside the chair. His hat was pushed down over his eyes and the faint sound of snores came from below its brim.

"Do something for you?" the man standing behind the counter asked, looking up from his work.

"I'd imagine so," Longarm replied, reaching into his coat pocket for the folded wallet that held his badge. He opened it and held it out for the deputy to inspect. The man behind the counter flicked his eyes over the badge and nodded.

"You'd be Custis Long, then? Deputy U.S. marshal?"

"Oh, I'm him, all right," Longarm assured the man. "And why I'm here is because I just had to shoot a man down in the saloon district. Figured I'd better report in to you about it, seeing I'm inside of your jurisdiction."

Now the deputy's expression changed. A frown formed on his face and his eyes widened as he gazed at Longarm before asking, "How long ago did this happen?"

"Not long. Less'n a half hour."

"Was this fellow you killed a prisoner of yours, or a man you were after?"

"Neither one. He was out to blackjack me, probably so he could rob me. He didn't know who I was, of course. He came at me with a slungshot while I was standing at the bar with my back to him."

"So you shot him?"

"He'd already landed one good whack on me," Longarm said. "I knew if he got in another one I'd be dead bait."

"I guess you better talk to the sheriff," the deputy said. Raising his voice, he called, "Sam! We got a case here you might like to take hold of."

Resettling his hat, this time in its proper place, the man who'd been dozing in the chair stood up. "What kinda case is it?" he asked the deputy.

"A killing. Down on saloon row. This fellow here's Custis Long. He's a deputy U.S. marshal outa Denver. Showed me his badge, so I guess he's who he says he is, all right."

"Well, Long," the sheriff went on as he turned to face Longarm and extend his hand, "I guess you already know who I am. If you didn't get my name, it's Sam Carter. Now, suppose you tell me the whys and wherefores. This man you shot, is he somebody you was after?"

Longarm shook his head. "Never saw him before. I was on the way down here, figuring to get acquainted with you and maybe get some idea of how the land lay to the north. That's where I'm headed. I stopped for a drink at a saloon called the Green Tree, and this fellow that jumped me looked like he'd passed out at one of the tables, so I didn't pay him much mind. I was standing at the bar when he came at me from behind, gave me a pretty good whack on the head, and was about to land another one when I drew and shot him."

"You're sure he jumped you first?"

"Ask the barkeep, he'll tell you if you think I'm spinning a yarn."

"Now, that's not what I'm doing, Long. I—" Carter paused and a thoughtful frown rippled over his face. "Long," he repeated. "U.S. marshal from Denver. You wouldn't be the man they call Longarm, would you?"

"It's a sorta nickname I answer to when somebody calls me by it," Longarm answered.

"Hell! I've heard about you, even way out here on the coast!" Carter exclaimed. "And from what I've heard, you don't need to do any explaining." He turned to his deputy and ordered, "Send the meat wagon over to the Green Tree. I'll write up the case after I've talked to Longarm for a minute." He faced Longarm and went on, "Let's go sit down in my office. You said you needed to know something about the country north of here and if I can help you out, I'll sure be glad to do it."

"Well, Sheriff Carter, I'm real obliged to you for all of what you've told me," Longarm said as he stood up. "I guess I know enough now that I don't have to worry about traipsing around in strange country, looking for things that ain't there."

"Just remember, it's easy to get turned around in the redwoods unless you stick to the logging trails. If you do get mixed up, all you've got to do is follow the evening sun to the ocean," Carter told him. "The old army road stays close to the shoreline. And I'm sorry I couldn't tell you more about the Indians, but I don't imagine they'll give you much trouble."

"I figure I can handle whatever I run into," Longarm said, his voice casual. "Now, I better be moseying along. I'd like to get an early start tomorrow morning, and it'll be nice to crawl into a bed that don't jiggle like a rocking chair all night and bust up my sleep."

Outside the courthouse, Longarm stood for a moment before turning his back and trying to walk away from the chilly night's breeze that was sweeping in from the bay. He started walking briskly, heading for his rooming house. Now and then a gust of the cold air roiling in from the bay struck him like a whirlwind, stabbing through his coat and trousers and bringing prickles to his skin.

"You better dig out some wool long johns before you start out in the morning, old son," Longarm told himself as he dug his hands deeper into his coat pockets. "And keep 'em on for the rest of the time you're up here in this damn windy place. But what you need right now is the sip of Tom Moore you missed getting when that fellow jumped you in the saloon. Seeing as how the place is on up ahead and on your way, you might just as well stop in and buy that bottle to take along, so you'll have a decent nightcap while you're here."

Reaching the corner of the saloon-lined street, Longarm turned into it and made his way to the Green Tree. No one was on either side of the bar and there was no body lying on the floor, but a bloodstain showed where the wide floorboards had been cleared of sawdust. Charley Hudson was sitting at one of the small tables that stood against the walls, his elbows on the table, his peg leg stuck out in front of him, his head held between his hands. He looked up when Longarm entered.

"Marshal Long!" he exclaimed. "I was hoping you'd be back! I was afraid I wouldn't have a chance to thank you for the help you've given me."

"Why, I wasn't doing nothing but my duty," Longarm told him. "I don't look for no thanks for that."

"Just the same, I could've been in trouble. The sheriff's pretty strict here, and when there's been a killing in a saloon he usually shuts the place down for two weeks afterward."

"He didn't say nothing about that to me," Longarm said.

"His men told me that when they came for the body," Hudson explained. "They told me who you are, too. No wonder you made such short work of that crook! And I owe you. Let me stand you a drink by way of thanks."

"I wouldn't say no to that," Longarm replied. "And I'd like to buy that whole bottle off of you, so I can take it along with me when I start tomorrow morning."

"That bottle's yours, it's sitting right there on the bar, and it won't cost you a dime. Since I've been sitting here thinking, I've changed my mind about being a saloon keeper. I'm going to lock this place up when I walk out of here tonight and go see if I can find a job in the woods tomorrow."

Longarm had already started for the bottle on the bar. Over his shoulder he said, "Now, don't let a little fracas put you off your course! And I reckon you've given some thought to—" He stopped, trying to find the kindest words possible to mention the difficulty of a man with only one leg finding a job in a lumber camp.

"I know," Hudson said for him. "There's not much a man with only one good leg can do around a logging stand. But I'll find something! I bet I can get hired on as a helper, or even if all I can get's just a swabby's job, I'll be better off doing what I know about than maybe going busted trying to run a saloon."

Longarm had poured his drink and was lifting it to his lips when the thought struck him. He replaced the brimming shot glass on the bar and turned back to face Hudson.

"What would you say if I offered you a job going along with me?" he asked.

"Going with you?" Hudson frowned. "But I'm not a lawman!"

"You don't have to be. This country's pretty strange to me, and I'd imagine you know it pretty good. You could keep me on the right trails and maybe help with a few chores when we stop and make camp and do, well, a passel of things that'd help me."

For a moment Hudson sat silent, his head bent down. When he looked up at Longarm he was grinning widely. He said, "It won't matter to me what I'd be doing. Marshal Long, you've just hired yourself a hand!"

Chapter 6

"These are the biggest trees I ever did see anywhere," Longarm remarked to Charley Hudson as their horses zig-zagged along the barely visible trail they were following through the grove of giant redwoods. "You reckon there's anyplace in the world where trees grow any bigger?"

"If there is, I've never heard about it," Hudson replied. "And there are plenty of places around here where you'll find redwoods even bigger than these."

Longarm looked around at the forest of giants through which the trail was winding. The boles of the biggest trees were twenty feet or more in diameter where they emerged from the hip-high tangle of vines and sprawling shrubs that covered the soft ground, and their tops seemed to reach to the low-lying clouds that shrouded the midmorning sky.

By Longarm's guess they were twenty or more miles inland on the sinuously winding trail they'd picked up a half day after riding out from Eureka.

Around them giant redwoods towered. The forest extended much farther than they could see. The thick and deeply striated reddish-brown bark of the massive trees soared upward, forming a shadowy guard for the trunks of saplings and other trees in the area. The leaves of the low-growing vegetation were dewed with glistening drops of water and the air seemed saturated with moisture, though the thick spongy duff under the hooves of their horses on the narrow trail was dry on the surface.

There had been stretches of the winding road—barely more than a trace in spots—where the duff that covered the trail had been cut into deep ruts by wagon wheels, and in such places Longarm had learned to look for an area where only the stumps of trees stood and the open sky was visible. Except for the few small fitful breezes that occasionally riffled the treetops and set them to sighing softly, the miles covered by Longarm and Charley Hudson had been largely silent.

Now as they came to one of the logged-over areas, Longarm remarked, "I'd sure hate to be sent out to cut down one of them big trees. But from these stumpy places we've been running across it don't seem to matter much to whoever tackles 'em."

"Felling a big redwood's not a one-man job, you know," Hudson said. "It takes a whole gang of loggers. There'll be maybe four saw-buckers and three or four wedgers and a half dozen swampies, and generally two or three flunkies. And that doesn't take in the trimmers and the teamsters, or the men that stay in camp to cook and keep the tools sharp and jobs like that. You'll likely run into sixty or seventy men in a big camp."

"Ain't that a pretty sizeable crew for just cutting down trees, even trees that get as big as these redwoods?"

"There are a lot more things done in a redwood logging camp than just cutting the trees," Hudson explained. "After they're felled the limbs have to be taken off, and the bottom branches are almost as big as most other kinds of trees. The trunks are usually too big to be moved, so they have to be split—some of them even quartered—before they can be hauled out to market."

"I figured this kind of logging was big business, but I didn't have any idea it was as big as you say," Longarm admitted. "I guess it draws plenty of men, though. It'd have to, to take care of all them jobs you rattled off."

"It's big enough to draw crooks, too," Hudson went on. "Most of the land up here still belongs to the government and it's not for sale. Big outfits like Dolbeer and Carson or the Excelsior Mills and rich men like Vance and McKay and Milford will take out a ten or twenty-year lease on two or three sections of standing redwood, maybe more. They'll set up a camp close to the middle of it and work it till all the merchantable timber's been cut. Then they'll move on to another place and do it all over again."

"I don't see anything crooked about that," Longarm ventured. "Not as long as they just take the trees off of the land they've paid for."

"That's what the legitimate operators like the ones that I just mentioned do," Hudson said. "The trouble's with the timber pirates—except that they like to call themselves 'claim crews.' They don't even buy timber rights leases, they just move in on a good stand of trees and start cutting. Then, as soon as they scalp off the prime trees they drop out of sight. My guess is, they scatter and lay low a while before they pop up someplace else, generally a pretty good distance away from where they were, and pull the same trick."

"Does anybody from the government ever try to stop 'em?"

"Not so's you'd notice."

Longarm was frowning as he said, "Seems to me there'd be somebody from the Interior Department out

63

here, keeping an eye on things like that. I guess you know the Interior bunch is the outfit in charge of things like government land."

"Yes. I know that," Hudson answered. Then a frown formed on his face as he went on, "The Interior Department might be in charge, but whoever's running it doesn't pay any attention to what's going on."

"I'm beginning to get that idea myself."

"I've worked on a lot of redwood stands, going on for ten years now," Hudson said slowly. "And I can tick off how many Interior Department inspectors I've seen all that time on the fingers of one hand and have three or four to spare."

"That sounds like somebody ain't tending to the business they're paid to look after," Longarm complained.

"If you want to narrow it down, Marshal Long, you're the first government man I've ever even heard about showing up out here where the tree pirates are working. And I'm not proud to say so, but there've been some tough times when I've worked for the timber pirates myself."

"Seems to me like a logging camp'd be a pretty hard thing to hide," Longarm said thoughtfully. "I'd guess there's a lot of money changing hands somewhere along the line."

"That's an old story up here, but redwood does bring top prices everywhere it's sold, Marshal. Those big trees saw out to the finest lumber you could ask for anywhere in the world."

"Now, that's something I didn't know."

Hudson went on, "After I couldn't hold up to working in the woods because of my leg, I put in some time in the office of the outfit that I was working for when I got hurt. The job didn't last long, but before they told me to draw down my time I handled bills of lading for outfits just about everywhere back East, and there were a lot from

64

England and France and Germany and Norway and Sweden and even for Russia."

"Well, that's neither here nor there. What I'm supposed to do is keep the Indians and the loggers from starting another war. But if my chief don't yank me back to Denver right away after my case is closed, I might just nose around a little bit and see what I can find out. It sure seems to me somebody oughta be doing something."

"Now that you've mentioned the Indians again, what about them?" Hudson asked. "I know they don't get along with the loggers, but there's not enough redskins left here along the coast anymore to make a very big fuss."

Longarm frowned thoughtfully as he said, "Maybe I've been too closemouthed about this case I'm on. I reckon you'd know more about it than I do right now."

"How are you going to help the Indians?" Hudson asked. "The quarrel between them and the loggers has been going on, well, almost since the first logging stand was opened twenty or so years ago."

"I ain't been able to figure out that part of it yet," Longarm admitted. "But from what I learned when I stopped at the Indian Bureau on the way here, some loggers have been throwing shots at the Indians for no reason. And the redskins say that about all they've got for food is the fish they catch, and they claim the loggers are ruining the fishing, with all the slash and trash they're dumping into the rivers. I ain't all that smart about fishing, but they tell me the fish swim up from the ocean to lay their eggs."

"Well, that's true enough," Hudson confirmed. "And that's when the Indians net them. But there are more and more logging stands being opened and the Indian tribes have been getting smaller for as long as I can remember. A few of them are down to just a handful of old men and women."

"If push comes to shove, I'd imagine there's enough

redskins left to put up a pretty good fight," Longarm said. "But I can't even start figuring the hows of this damned case until I find some Indians and listen to their side of the fuss."

"We're heading in the right direction, then. Most of the Indians have been pushed up into the Klamath River country by now."

"How far away's that from where we are now?" Longarm asked.

"Three or four days, if we take our time."

"I guess we'll pass by some places where they're cutting trees?"

"Of course. There are, oh, I'd say a half dozen logging stands between here and the mouth of the Klamath River."

"You'll likely know some of the men that'll be working in 'em, I'd imagine?"

"It'd be a real surprise if all we ran into was strangers," Hudson replied. "Most loggers have itchy feet. They don't generally stay with one outfit very long."

"Let's just stop for a while at the first logging camp we run across, then," Longarm told his companion. "Once I've had a chance to do a little nosing around, maybe I'll get a better idea of what I'm going up against."

Longarm reined in and Charley Hudson followed his example. He looked questioningly at Longarm and asked, "Is something wrong?"

"Not that I know of. But I heard some kinda noise a minute ago, and just now I heard it again."

Cocking his head, Hudson turned from side to side, listening. Then he said, "You've got better ears than I have. What you've been hearing is axes. We're close to where loggers are at work, and if we get to the stand in time you'll get a chance to watch them bring down a tree."

"You think we can get to wherever it is in time to see it?" Longarm asked.

Hudson shook his head. "Probably not. My guess is that we're still at least a half mile away from where that timber crew's working, and the tree's just about to fall."

When the faraway sounds ended abruptly there was a short period of silence, disturbed only by a few shouts that had been reduced by the distance to an almost unidentifiable whisper of sound. Suddenly the undistinguishable whispers of voices were drowned by an ominous creaking and crackling. The high-pitched creaking seemed to go on forever, then a salvo of sharp cracks, almost like rifle shots, broke the air. Suddenly the sharp cracks were replaced by a booming thud that seemed to explode and echo through the forest, then the air was still.

"Now you know what a big redwood tree sounds like when it falls," Hudson told Longarm. "The axmen and the trimmers will be going to work in a minute or two and they'll make enough noise to guide us to the logging stand."

"I heard enough noise just then to last me for a spell," Longarm said. "That must've been one hell of a big tree that they just cut down."

"I'd say it was about average," Hudson replied. "Maybe a hundred and fifty feet high, by the sound of it when it toppled. That'd make it maybe twenty or twenty-five feet at the base."

"You mean you can tell all that just from listening?" Longarm asked.

"You could, too, if you'd seen as many redwoods felled as I have," Hudson said, smiling. Ahead of them the ringing of axes was beginning to sound. He gestured toward the forest that still stretched in front of them and went on, "I guess you can hear the axmen. It's just like listening to somebody talk when you understand the language they're using."

"When you put it that way, I guess it makes sense," Longarm said. "Until I learned how to listen to footsteps I couldn't tell whether whoever was making 'em was big or little, or whether they were barefoot or wearing boots."

He fell silent as the metallic ringing of axes reached their ears, and before he could say anything else the ringing of still more axes added to the din.

"That don't sound so far off," Longarm said.

"It's not. Maybe a half mile or so. Good ears are better than good eyes along these forest trails where the cover's as thick as it is."

Although they sped up, another half hour passed before Longarm and Hudson came within view of the lumber gang that was working on the felled redwood tree. The scene was a busy one. A dozen or more men were at work along the tree's huge bole. Two teams, one on either side of the felled giant, were hammering platforms together, while others were spaced out along the trunk.

Those near the tip of the tree were swinging axes, chopping off the branches. From the top point where the branches ended down to the raw brownish-red butt, two axmen who had climbed atop the trunk were chopping away at the thick, deeply striated bark to form lines around the tree trunk's massive girth.

"They're marking for saw cuts," Hudson explained to Longarm as they reined in a short distance from the busy scene. Pointing to the ax wielders on the huge tree trunk he went on, "A ten- or twelve-foot section from the butt is about all an ox team can drag. They'll space the cut lines farther apart as they work toward the top."

Near the butt of the fallen giant, a pair of sawyers were mounting an already completed platform. One of them dragged an end of a twenty-foot saw. His partner leaped from the platform to the bole of the tree and stood waiting while his partner hauled the twenty-foot bucksaw to the platform's top and slid one end within reach.

Balancing the foot-wide sawblade between them, the pair set the sawteeth on the line scored into the bark and began bucking the saw. It cut into the massive trunk with a high-pitched sound that to Longarm's ears sounded like a wordless song, so smooth was the tempo of their sawing.

At one side of the felled tree and a little distance from it, oxen were being hitched into teams by another group of busy workers. It was a scene of organized confusion, and in his mind Longarm compared it to a band of cowhands cutting a big steer herd into manageable bunches.

"They sure don't waste any time," he remarked to his companion. "How far'll they have to drag them big chunks of tree?"

"Not very far. There's sure to be a skid road close by, and the teams will pick it up and get the logs to the Klamath River. They'll finish trimming whatever branch stubs are left on the trunk, and peel the bark off the sections. Then they'll roll them into the river."

"And just let 'em float from there down to the ocean?" Longarm asked.

"They won't float until high water, after the rains start. By then there'll be rivermen waiting at the mouth of the river to look after them. They'll raft the logs up and tow them to the sawmills down by Eureka. They'll go right through the mill, and as soon as they're cut into boards they'll be stacked in the drying yards."

"Damned if I don't think lumbering's worse than ranching," Longarm observed, gazing at the activity around the bole of the giant redwood. Men were swarming over its huge length now, and axes were ringing near the top of the felled tree. "At least a cowhand gets to sit in his saddle while he's working."

"You've got a point there," Hudson admitted. "But when you come down to it, a timber crew's not all that much different from a ranch. They're both a bunch of men working on a job together, even if the jobs aren't anywhere near alike."

"Well, if it's just the same to you, I'll climb up as far as the next man as long as I can keep pretty near the ground," Longarm told him. "Sitting here in the saddle's just about as high up as I'd care to get."

"Then you—" Hudson broke off before he finished his remark and jerked his head toward a husky man who'd left the last of the working crews and was making his way toward them. He went on, "We're going to have a little visit from the boss."

"That fellow coming up to us?" Longarm asked. "I take it you know him?"

"Too damned well, and he doesn't like me any better than I like him. He's Bull Kestell. I guess he's got a proper first name, but I've never heard it. All I really know about him is that he's meaner than a pack of wildcats."

By this time the man approaching was near enough to hail them. In a hoarse voice he called, "You two! If you're looking for jobs we ain't got any, and we don't feed strangers. Just turn around and push off before you get underfoot of these men who're trying to work!"

"Now, we ain't close enough to get in nobody's way," Longarm replied.

He was studying the approaching man as he spoke. Kestell was both tall and broad, with high chubby cheekbones that pushed his eyelids into slits. He wore an unbuttoned vest over a blue denim shirt, and the beginning of a potbelly pushed the vest out. His brown covert-cloth trousers were tucked into calf-high boots.

Longarm went on, "We just happened to be riding by

when we heard that big tree fall over, so we figured we'd stop and take a look-see."

"You've been here long enough to see all you need to," the logger said. "Longer than you've got any business to be."

Kestell was close enough now for Longarm to see that only one side of his mouth opened when he talked. Before Longarm could reply Kestell recognized Hudson and the corners of his mouth turned down still further.

Gruffly, he went on, "We ain't hard up enough to hire cripples, Hudson. I don't know who your friend here is, but I don't want either one of you around. Now get moving!"

Longarm glanced quickly from the corners of his eyes at his companion. Hudson was staring angrily at Kestell, his right hand posed on his thigh, his fingers spread in readiness to grab for the holstered revolver at his hip. Kestell had not taken his eyes off Hudson. His hand was also clawed in preparation for a draw.

This was not the first time Longarm had faced a similar dilemma, and he realized quite well that it was no time for a gunfight to start. Once a shot was fired, the men of Kestell's logging crew could be expected to join in, and he'd already noticed that a number of them were wearing gun belts. The nearest loggers had stopped work and were staring at their boss as he faced the two strangers.

"Don't do it, Charley!" Longarm said to Hudson. He spoke barely louder than a whisper and did not take his eyes off the logging boss. Then, raising his voice he called to Kestell, "And don't you go for your gun, either! My name's Long. I'm a United States marshal and this man's working for me. If you start pushing too hard, you'll know mighty quick what trouble means!"

"I guess you can prove who you are?" Kestell challenged.

71

"Sure," Longarm said smoothly. "Now, I'm going to take my badge outa my pocket, if that's what you got a hankering to see. But if you move that gun of yours a single inch, I can get my Colt out a damn sight faster than my badge. You understand that?"

"All I want is to look at your badge, if you've got one," Kestell replied. His voice no longer held a challenge.

Lifting his wallet from his pocket, Longarm flipped it open to display his badge. Kestell studied it and nodded.

"All right," he said. "But unless you got official business on this stand, that badge don't mean a thing. If you've got any business to talk, get it off your chest. If you haven't got any, then just turn your nags and ride off."

Longarm had no intention of prolonging what had become an unpleasant situation, one that could quickly explode into open violence. However, he'd been a lawman for enough years to recognize the nagging undertone of unease in Kestell's voice. It was not the first time he'd sensed such worry, and he made a mental note to check into the man's background when time allowed.

Turning to Hudson, Longarm jerked his head toward the trail. He waited for his companion to start, then reined his own mount around and followed.

Chapter 7

"I don't generally turn my back and walk away from a man like Bull Kestell," Longarm told Hudson after they'd gotten out of earshot of the loggers. "But this wasn't no time to be starting a fracas. I wasn't sent here all the way from Denver to take a bully like him down a peg or two."

"In my book, there's times when it takes as much guts to walk away from a fight than to take one on," Hudson agreed. "That damn Bull Kestell's got a permanent chip on his shoulder, though. He'd sooner fight than eat, even if he was starving."

"It was easy enough to see that you and him wasn't exactly strangers," Longarm went on. "I guess you know him from someplace where you worked before?"

"We've been on the same stand, oh, three times, as I recall," Hudson replied. "And in a, well, call it in a backward sort of way, he's partly responsible for me being a damn cripple right now."

"Oh? How's that?" Immediately, Longarm was sorry

he'd asked the question. He'd already sensed that his companion was very conscious of his affliction, and quickly added, "Or would you rather not talk about it?"

"I've gotten past the time when I'd back away from talking about having just one good leg," Hudson said.

Being careful to keep his voice neutral, Longarm said, "If you got a mind to talk, I'm listening."

After a moment of thoughtful silence, Hudson went on, "Bull was the woods foreman on the last stand where I lumberjacked. He was my boss, of course. The first thing he did was to partner me off with a crony of his. Jake Blake, he said his name was, but the first time or two I called him by it he acted like he'd never heard it before."

When Hudson stopped for breath, Longarm asked him, "You figured this friend of Kestell's for a crook?"

"Maybe it's just that I'm carrying a grudge against him for the shape I'm in now, but he was a chum of Bull Kestell's, and Bull's name is down in my book as a no-good son of a bitch from the word go."

"You got brains enough not to talk wild, Charley," Longarm said. "I could see that five minutes after you and me swapped hellos back in that saloon you was figuring to run. That wasn't all I could see, either. You ain't the kind to bad-mouth a man just because you and him don't get along."

"Well, I'm glad to know how you feel. But going back to where we were a minute ago, I could tell in a minute that this fellow Blake never had done any woods work."

"You're telling me that Bull Kestell had hired a man that couldn't pull his own weight on the job, just because they was friends or something?"

Nodding, Hudson went on, "After I'd worked with this Jake Blake for about half a day, I told Bull that his friend didn't know his ass from a hot rock about logging, but he

74

wouldn't listen. I told him I'd rather partner up with a better man and he told me to go to hell."

"Then I guess you and him got in a fracas and your leg got hurt so bad they had to take it off?"

"No, it wasn't like that," Hudson replied. "A day or so later Blake and me were trimming a big redwood and he wasn't watching what he was doing. He made a wild swing with his ax and took off my foot instead of the branch he was supposed to be aiming at."

Longarm nodded as he said, "I can see why you blame Kestell for what happened. And just from that little bit I saw of him back there, I can't say I blame you."

"I guess I'm about halfway to blame, myself." Hudson's voice was rueful. "If I'd had any sense I'd've drawn down my time and found a job on another stand. But that's past and gone and there's no use picking at old scabs. I try not to think about it or feel sorry for myself anymore."

They rode on in silence, reached the road and turned their horses north. After they'd covered a half mile or so, Longarm turned to Hudson.

"You know a lot more about this part of the country than I do," he said. "And a lot more about timbering, too. I hope it ain't going to bother you if I ask you questions now and again. And I don't mean just how to get someplace. I got to know more about the people I'm up against."

"When I told you I'd come along and do what I could to give you a hand, I didn't tie any strings to it. Ask me what you want to. You'll sure get my honest answer."

"Let's start with Bull Kestell, then," Longarm said. "I got the notion when I was talking to him back there that he'd've given the rough edge of his tongue to anybody who happened to stop by. He acted like he just didn't want nobody at all watching what him and his crew were doing."

"If you're wondering whether he's a timber pirate, I'd say the chances are that he is. He might be working that stand on his own, but I'd be inclined to think he's running it for somebody else."

"You don't know whether he's ever struck out on his own before?"

"He never had, from what I gathered," Hudson replied. "A woods boss draws top dollar, but I can't see how Bull could've put up enough money to meet the payroll of a crew as big as the one working that stand of trees."

Longarm nodded. "I was getting around to asking you that. I started wondering when I saw that big bunch of lumberjacks, and all the gear they had."

"It's not any of my business, but why'd you leave so tame?" Hudson frowned. "You carry a badge, and I know you didn't want a fight, but you've got the right to ask him to show you his timber lease."

"There's more'n one reason why I didn't push," Longarm replied. "First one is that I already got a case with them redskins to handle, and I'm duty-bound to close it before I take on a new one."

"Sure. I can see that," Hudson said, nodding.

Longarm went on, "Another reason is that I'd need to find out more'n I know now about that Bull Kestell. My hunch is that he wouldn't be operating so wide open unless he's in cahoots with somebody that's on the inside track."

"Hell, Longarm, everybody that's worked for even a little while on these redwood stands knows how much tree pirating is going on. And everybody knows there's payoffs changing hands."

"I've seen the likes before," Longarm agreed. "Not in the timber business, maybe, but in gold mining and cattle ranching and all like that. But the thing is, when I set out to make a case, I've got to come up with proof that a judge and jury will believe."

"How're you ever going to prove something like a payoff?" Hudson asked. "When money changes hands under the table, the men who're handling it make sure there aren't any witnesses."

"Oh, I've worked on a case or more when I've been able to prove there was payoffs. But I can tell you this, Charley, proving there was a payoff made sure ain't no easy job."

"Yes, I can see that."

They rode on in silence for a while, then Longarm asked, "How much farther do we have to go before we need to keep our eyes peeled for them Indians we're trying to find?"

"Quite a ways. I picked out this road—if you can call it that—because it's easier traveling than any of the trails farther inland. You'll see what I'm talking about when we fork east toward the Klamath River."

"I don't guess there're any towns along the way we're going, then."

"Not real towns. A few sawmills, but they're mostly right on the shore. It makes loading lumber easier, and there's any number of little coves where the water's calm and where a ship or two can find safe harbor to take on a load."

"Well, I ain't learned a lot about this part of the country yet," Longarm said, "but there's one thing I'm sure of. It ain't like anything I've ever seen before, and I don't reckon I'll ever see the likes of it anyplace else."

"You're right about that," Hudson agreed. "But there's something about it that keeps people here regardless of the rough country and the bad weather. I left it a time or two, but every time I did I found myself coming back, so finally I decided the best thing I could do was stay."

For the next hour or so they rode on along the winding trail in companionable silence. There were fewer big redwood groves now, and in those that they passed through the trees were smaller and less numerous than the giants in the

77

stands they'd encountered earlier. The trail narrowed and the tracks of wagon wheels were visible less often.

Looking at the green terrain in front of them as they were making their way through one of the groves, Longarm blinked and then frowned. Turning to Hudson he asked, "I ain't real sure yet, but ain't that water I see shining right up ahead?"

"It is. That's Big Lagoon," Hudson replied.

"Ain't a lagoon about the same as a lake, Charley?"

"Pretty much. And there's another one farther along, but they aren't anything to worry about. All you need to do is hold in your horse so it won't try to go too fast while we're crossing them."

"Just what do you mean, crossing?" Longarm frowned. "I can swim if I've got to, but I can't say it's something I enjoy doing."

"You won't have to swim. And you can see from here how far we'd have to ride to get around it."

"Wait a minute, now," Longarm protested. "Going by what I can see from here, that's a lot of water. How big is that thing, anyhow?"

"Oh, a couple of miles long and a mile or so wide. The one up ahead of it's bigger, though."

Longarm turned back to the lagoon and studied its wide surface carefully for several minutes. As he returned his attention to Hudson he was shaking his head.

"Charley, you better tell me if I heard you right. You said we don't have to swim, so I reckon you mean we're going to ride our nags across. Am I right?"

"It's the easiest way, Longarm," Hudson replied. "We'd run into a lot of rough going if we rode around them. The stretch between them and the ocean is all cut-up rocks, and on the land side there's several sharp drop-offs and some other pretty tricky places to look out for."

"Well," Longarm said resignedly, "you know the country and I don't. If you're man enough to ride a horse across that stretch of water, I reckon the least I can do is trail along. Just be sure you keep ahead of me, and I'll make sure my nag don't step to either side."

"All you have to do is keep your horse as close as you can behind mine," Hudson told him. "I'll guarantee that you won't get into any trouble. You won't even get your feet wet. The water's too shallow to reach up to your horse's belly."

By this time they'd moved into a curve in the trail, and the trees ahead had thinned enough to give Longarm a broader view of the landscape. The water of the lagoon looked dark and foreboding, and on his left, across a strip of rock-studded sand beyond it he could see the roiled sparkling waves of the Pacific.

In contrast, the water in the lagoon was totally placid. Here and there some small tangles of bushes rose above its surface and the charred lightning-blasted boles of a few small trees rose above the narrow edges. In addition to the sweep of water just ahead he could now see a second expanse beyond it.

"I guess you know what you're doing," he told Hudson. "So just go on ahead. I'll follow right behind you."

Hudson nodded without turning to look back as his horse stepped into the water. Longarm watched him as he moved out into the lagoon. Just as he'd promised, the water's surface remained only a few inches above the animal's fetlocks and stayed well below its knees. Even Hudson's feet in the stirrups were several inches above the lagoon's surface.

Giving his companion time to advance a dozen yards, Longarm toed his horse ahead. The animal did not balk, but stepped into the water. Though Longarm kept a tighter grip on the reins than was his habit, the horse moved readily and forged steadily ahead. Though their progress was slow, the wide expanse was soon behind them, and ahead he could see rays of sunshine dancing on the surface of the second lagoon.

To Longarm's surprise, Hudson reined away from the lagoon ahead. Touching his horse's belly with his toe, Longarm soon caught up with his companion.

"Ain't we going across that other pond up ahead?" he asked.

Hudson shook his head. "No. If we were in a hurry and heading on up the coast, we would. But there's a pretty fair trail inland from here. It starts just a couple of miles up ahead, and it's the easiest way to get to the Klamath River without following the coast another five or six days to the river mouth."

"And you're pretty sure that we'll run into some Indians if we take this cross-country trail?"

"This is an old Indian trail," Hudson explained. "It ends at the Klamath, right at the place where the Indians do most of their fishing."

"Let's get going on it, then," Longarm said. "I can't do much on this case till I find some redskins. Time's been passing, and I ain't been keeping up with it because of all the lallygagging around I've had to do. Now, I got to get down to business."

"How come this is called a creek when it's just about as big as most of them rivers we've run into?" Longarm asked.

"That's something I don't know," Hudson answered. "As I understand it, when old Josiah Gregg led his bunch of explorers along here fifty or so years ago, they gave names to most of the streams along this part of the coast. Sometimes they just kept to the names the Indians called them, other times they tagged them with any name that they fancied."

"So they called this one Redwood Creek because of all the trees that were growing around it."

"It was likely the first stand of redwoods they'd run into. They'd been traveling down from the north. On farther up, toward the Oregon country, the big redwoods peter out."

Longarm looked along the wide course of the bubbling swift stream where they'd reined in. Its surface was dotted with strings of frothy foam that roiled on the water's surface. Here and there he could see the dark bulges of boulders on the creek's bed. The stumps of dozens of redwood trees that had been felled on both sides of its bed rose thickly above the tops of the high waving grasses that covered the ground for a half mile or more on each side of the watercourse.

"A man can see right easy that there was sure a nice stand of redwood trees along here," he said. "And I don't guess they'd been cut when the first white men passed by. But we got better things to do than look at the scenery, and the first thing is to get on across this river and get on our way."

"Not river," Hudson told him. "Creek. It's called Redwood Creek, and it looks a lot bigger than it is, but it's not big enough or deep enough to be a river."

"It'd sure qualify for a river most places I've seen."

"Appearances can fool you, Longarm. It's wide and the bottom's rocky, but it's shallow. We won't have any trouble riding across it."

"Let's get started, then," Longarm told him. "From what I recall you saying, it's still a pretty good ways to that river we're heading for."

"It is. Not that we've got so many miles to cover before we get to the Klamath, but that stretch of high brush on the other side of the creek's not as wide as it looks to be. After we get past it we'll be starting up a rocky slope where the going gets pretty rough."

"You've been across here before, so I reckon you know what the bottom's like," Longarm said. "Go on ahead, Charley. I'll be right in back of you."

Hudson toed his horse into motion and reined it toward the water's edge. The animal stepped into the shallows and slowly began high-footing across the white-frothed stream. After the animal had taken its first hesitating steps, Longarm saw that the water here was no deeper than that in the lagoon had been.

Longarm watched Hudson's slow progress and waited until the other man's mount had made its slow careful way a few yards into the stream, then reined his own mount into the water. The horse took a few steps forward and stopped. It lowered its head to drink and Longarm slacked the reins. He was not prepared for the animal to rear and wheel and almost throw him when a shot rang out from the brush beyond the water's edge ahead and a bullet sent up a spout of water between his horse and Hudson's.

Longarm did not have to search for a target as he whipped his Winchester from its saddle scabbard. A puff of yellowish powder smoke had risen from a clump of brush twenty or thirty yards beyond the opposite bank of the stream following the shot.

Wise in the ways of bushwhackers, Longarm did not aim at the exact spot marked by the plume of gunsmoke. Instead, he bracketed the bush with two quick shots, one on either side of the point where the gunsmoke was slowly dissipating in the light breeze. Flicking his eyes toward Hudson, he saw that his companion had drawn his revolver and was raising it, his gaze fixed on the bush where their unknown attacker had taken cover.

Longarm knew nothing about Hudson's skill with a pistol or, for that matter, in gunfighting. He called to his companion, "Put a couple of shots in the middle of them bushes! I'll take care of the sides!"

Even before Longarm had finished speaking the bark of Hudson's revolver split the air. Longarm had already levered a fresh shell into his Winchester. He loosed another now, seconds before a second shot boomed from the clump of brush and another yellowish cloud rose above it to merge with the thinned, still dissipating powder smoke from the first shot. Skittering across the surface of the stream between Longarm and Hudson, the bullet clunked with a dull splatting sound into a big stone on the opposite bank.

Longarm was positive now that whoever was shooting at them was armed with a long-outdated rifle. The first shot had started him thinking, and now the second confirmed his conclusions. The dull flat report of the first shot when it was fired, the long interval between it and the second, and the sullen splat of the bullet when it hit the boulder, combined to convince him that the shots could only have come from a muzzle loader.

Raising his voice, he called, "Whoever you are over there, we ain't here to hurt nobody! We're just traveling through! Hold your fire and let's have a parlay before somebody gets hurt!"

"Are you crazy, Longarm?" Hudson called. "Whoever that is over there shot first, and it looks to me like he means business! Damn it, don't let's take any fool chances!"

"Maybe it's a chance and maybe it ain't," Longarm called back. "Just don't holster your gun, and I'll hold mine aimed in case whoever that is don't do what I figure he might!"

"It's likely some fool Indian who don't even understand what you said to him!" Hudson protested.

"Well, whoever it is, he's had plenty of time to shoot

again, but he ain't done it," Longarm pointed out. "And it'd likely be an Indian that's doing the shooting, because a redskin's the only one I can think of who'd still be toting the kind of old black-powder muzzle loader them shots came from!"

"Do you make surrender?" a man's voice called from the bush clump. "Say so now or I shoot you some more!"

Longarm raised his voice and called, "If you don't shoot us, we won't shoot you!"

"This you make to promise?" the invisible shootist called back.

"We sure do," Longarm answered. "But how about us riding on up to the bank now?"

"Nyet!" the still invisible man shouted loudly. "You stay in river! Throw guns in vater! Then ve talk!"

"What the hell was that he said first?" Hudson asked.

"Whatever it was, it sure sounded to me like he said no," Longarm replied. Raising his voice again, he went on, "How about if we come on to shore and lay down our guns? No use ruining 'em, throwing 'em in the water."

"You geeve parole?" the man in the brush called.

"If you mean what I think you do, you got our word on it!" Longarm agreed.

"Do, then," the man replied.

Longarm and Hudson nudged their horses into motion. When they reached the bank, Longarm swung out of his saddle and laid his Winchester on the rocky bank. He gestured with his head for Hudson to do the same, and when he did so, raised his voice again.

"All right," he called. "We've put our guns down. Now how about you coming out and laying yours down, too?"

"Is a thing more," the still hidden man called back. "You tell me both of you that you are surrender to army of Nicholas, Czar of all the Russias!"

Chapter 8

"Did what he said make any sense to you?" Hudson asked. His bewilderment was apparent from the tone of his voice.

"Not a bit. Whoever that is in them bushes is crazy. That's what I suspected right after he began yelling at us."

"What're we going to do about him? Even if we have put our rifles down, he's as likely as not to shoot us!"

"He don't sound all that bad to me, and I've run into a few like him before now."

"How in hell can we trust a crazy man?"

"Well, now," Longarm replied, "so far we've talked him outa shooting us, so let's go along and see what he wants. It won't hurt us none. But I sure don't aim to give up my Colt, even if it means using it."

"I guess we're in so deep now, all we can do is go ahead," Hudson said. "Go on. Tell him we'll give up to the Russian czar."

Raising his voice again, Longarm called, "We've done surrendered, and I don't guess it makes much never-mind whether it's to you or to whoever's the big boss in Russia. Come on out and let's have a little parlay."

In the heavy patch of brush in front of them there was a stirring of leaves and branches. Then a man rose slowly from the undergrowth. For a moment or so all that Longarm and Hudson could do was to stare at the strange apparition that emerged. The man with the long grizzled black-and-white beard who stood up and stepped away from the bushes was stocky, and his strange garb made him look even stockier.

A flat-topped cap without a bill covered the new arrival's head. The top of the cap was made of leather, which must at one time have been red, but was now faded to a dull pink and spiderwebbed with tiny cracks. A leather greatcoat fell from his shoulders to his ankles. Like the cap, it was worn and cracked, its surface dulled by time and weather.

Over the coat the stranger had on a wide leather belt that had originally been white but was now yellowed and criss-crossed with the tiny lines of aging. A shoulder harness supported the belt, the harness straps crossing in an X over his chest. He carried a long-barreled flintlock, its stock dull and scored by cracks, its barrel rusted.

"I am Alexis Viatsolof," he announced. Though his voice was shrill and tinny with age and his English thickly accented, neither Longarm nor Hudson had any difficulty understanding him. He went on, "Soldier from the Ninth Caucasus Regiment of the Army of Czar Nicholas. Your parole I vill take, and you my prisoners vill be. You vill do as I say, or I shoot you."

"Hold on just a damn minute!" Longarm exclaimed. "You ain't in Russia now! You're in America, and this czar you keep talking about's been dead for I don't know how long. There's a fellow called Alexander that's in charge over there now."

"Lies!" the man exclaimed shrilly. "You lie to me like do other Amerikanski! But even if vat you say is true, I vill serve Nicholas's son as I did him!"

In a whisper, Hudson said to Longarm, "You sure hit it right when you figured this fellow's a crazy."

"Oh, he's crazy, all right," Longarm said. "I had him tabbed right off. That's why I said what I did just now. Back in Eureka when I had that little talk with Sheriff Carter I told you about, he told me a lot of things I didn't rightly need to know. Before I steered him right, he was talking about places like that old fort the Russians had built on the coast a ways to the south, when they were laying claim to Alaska and a lot of America."

"Fort Ross?" Hudson frowned. "I've heard about it, but I never have been there. You suppose that fellow was left behind when the Russian army moved out and went home?"

"I figure he's got to be."

"Well, it makes sense, in a way. But what in hell do we do next?"

"That's what I've been trying to puzzle out since I began to stall him."

"I sort of figured that's what you were doing," Hudson said. "But I still don't see why we've got to stall."

"Crazy folks can be right helpful sometimes," Longarm said thoughtfully. "All that's wrong with 'em is, they don't play by nobody's rules but their own. Now, that fellow over there, you can tell from what he's said that he's a week late and a dollar short, but we're just asking for trouble we don't need if we get into a showdown."

"You mean you're really going to give in to him?"

"I figure there's got to be somebody helping him, and it's more than likely Indians. You know how they are, figuring that crazy people bring luck because they're sorta holy. Remember, Charley, it's Indians I was sent here to look for. This might be an easy way to find a bunch of 'em."

There was doubt in Hudson's voice when he spoke again after a brief thoughtful silence. "Well," he said, "you're the boss. Whatever you say, I'll go along with you. But if—"

Hudson broke off when Viatsolof called loudly, "Too long you talk! I vait no more! Go from your guns avay!"

"I guess we better," Longarm said. "But remember, if he tries to take our pistols away from us, all bets are off. He'll be close enough so we can jump him by then."

Longarm took two long steps away from the rifles he and his companion had put on the ground. After hesitating for a moment, Hudson followed him. They stood motionless, looking toward the Russian.

"Is good," their captor said. "Take now the horses and come to me closer."

Keeping his voice low as they moved to pick up the reins of their horses, Longarm said to Hudson, "This is working out better'n I figured. Move around to the offside of your nag, like I aim to do. If we stay up close against our horses and keep 'em between him and us, there's a chance he won't even notice that we've got on our gun belts."

Walking abreast, leading their horses, Longarm and Hudson walked slowly up to the old man. As they drew closer they realized for the first time how ancient he really was.

Viatsolof's white beard was thin and straggling, and through its sparse growth a maze of deeply incised wrinkles was visible. The lines covered his cheeks and chin and his lips were crisscrossed with equally deep lines. His sparse eyebrows were as thin as the beard, and the whites of his deep blue eyes were almost hidden by a network of tiny red veins. For all that, he stood erect and moved easily but very slowly toward them as they approached.

"You are surrender now to me, nyet?" he asked.

"Why, I reckon you can call it that if you got a mind to," Longarm replied. "Me and my friend don't aim to fight you, but we want to know what you got in mind to do if we stay peaceful."

"To my peoples I veel take you."

"They're Russian, I take it, like you are?"

"Nyet." The oldster shook his head. "Indians, they are. You veel come veeth me, is small vay to vere they stay. I talk veeth council, then I tell you."

"Don't you reckon we better step back and get our rifles?" Longarm suggested. "Might be they'd come in handy."

Viatsolof did not reply for a moment but stood with a small frown of indecision flitting across his face. Then he pointed to Hudson and said, "*Da*. You fetch." As he spoke he raised the stock of the long muzzle loader and cradled the weapon in his arm. Watching him, Longarm felt sure that the old soldier had reloaded his weapon before emerging from cover.

Hudson glanced at Longarm, who nodded. Then he took the few steps necessary to reach the rifles and returned carrying them. Longarm noticed that he shielded his gun and holster by carrying the rifles low in the crook of his arm. Without waiting for orders from their captor, Hudson put the rifles in the saddle scabbards.

Nodding, Viatsolof swept the muzzle of his rifle in a small arc. He said, "Go. Valk in front from me. I am lead horses, I tell you vere to go."

Longarm nodded to Hudson. They edged past the old man. As they passed him both men turned to look back.

Viatsolof was gathering the reins of the horses and looping them around one arm. He started following them, his ancient rifle cradled in the crook of his free arm. When he looked up and saw Longarm and Hudson gazing at him, he brought the muzzle of his rifle up an inch or so.

"I vatch," he told them. "You run, I shoot."

"Damned if I don't think he means it," Hudson said in a loud whisper to Longarm.

"You just bet he does," Longarm agreed. Raising his voice, he asked Viatsolof. "Which way you want us to go?"

Scanning the landscape ahead of them, the old soldier raised the muzzle of his ancient rifle and pointed to a grove of trees a quarter mile or so away. Beyond the trees a long range of low hills showed as a line of green humps on the horizon.

"Go so," Viatsolof told them. "Middle of trees."

Nodding, Longarm turned and started walking slowly in the direction their captor had indicated. After they'd walked a short distance he glanced back over his shoulder. Viatsolof was several paces behind him. He had looped the reins of the two horses over his shoulder and gripped his rifle in both hands. He carried the weapon at a slant across his chest, where he could shoulder it quickly.

Without turning his head toward Hudson, Longarm cautioned his companion, "Don't look back, Charley. It might make that old geezer nervous, and he's ready to use that gun he's toting."

"Where you figure he's taking us?" Hudson asked in a half whisper.

"Damned if I know," Longarm replied. "At a guess, I'd say he's herding us toward that group of Indians he mentioned."

"That makes sense," Hudson pointed out. "He did say something about a council."

"From what he's said, I'm hoping real strong that he's been running with one of them Indian tribes we're looking for." Longarm's voice matched the low-pitched half whisper in which Hudson had spoken. He went on, "All we can hope for is that they've got the same peaceful intentions we do. If they don't, we'll have to get free of 'em. But we'll jump off of that bridge when we come to it."

"He's sure old," Hudson said after a moment of silence. "I hope I got as much get up and go when I get to be his age."

"I've been doing some figuring in my head," Longarm replied. "As close as I can recall, them Russians that had tried to settle down here in California got run home damn near fifty years ago. This old geezer must've been a full-grown man by then, or he sure couldn't've been one of their soldiers."

"Then he's at least seventy years old or better!"

Longarm nodded. "Something like that. But he's still got most of his wits about him, even if he don't make good sense now and again."

"He's not the first old fellow that's held together a long time," Hudson observed. "I've seen loggers damn near as old as him, and maybe a few of them are older. But they swing an ax or buck a saw along with fellows half their age."

Longarm nodded. "My job keeps me moving pretty good, and I see some cowhands now and then that're as old as this fellow. They're just about as spry, too."

"Too much you talk!" Viatsolof called. "Make no more, now! I do not hear vat you say, maybe you talk to find vay of getting free. Now you be quiet!"

Longarm risked a low whisper, "One thing you got to give that old boy credit for. He's got a lot of years behind him, but he still ain't no slouch at what he's doing. I figure when he was pulled into the Russian army he had some real good teachers, whoever they was."

They plodded ahead, silent now as Viatsolof led their horses weaving in and out on the almost invisible path between the trees. In front of them they still saw nothing but sky between the closely spaced pine boles. The pine stand thinned as they drew closer to the edge of the grove, and now the jagged rim of the plateau they'd been crossing since putting the lagoons behind them was visible between the tree trunks.

In the far distance the jagged peaks of mountains pierced a blue cloudless sky. They approached the rim of the level meadowlike land beyond the pine grove. Now still more features of the vast expanse between them and the faraway line of mountain peaks became visible.

Below them the flanks of high rugged hills were divided by the wide blue line of a river. The water flowed through a narrow green-wooded strip at the bottom of a canyon. Its surface was broken by long stretches of roiling white foam. In many of the expanses of foam the brownish-black knobs of boulders rose above the surface of the water.

Finally the last narrow stretch of the level grassed land was behind them, and when they reached the rim of the canyon they put aside thoughts of the man to whom they'd surrendered and stood gazing at the broadly gaping canyon through which the foam-capped river ran.

At a lower level on the opposite side of the river another rock shelf jutted from the sloping yellow-white flank of a higher cliff. Beyond its rim the rocky rounded rims of still more cliffs were visible. Trees mounted the slopes and stood on the shelving rock ledges where they jutted widely enough to support growth, but they were not the towering redwoods that grew on the coastal plain. These were almost domelike cedars, with broad bases and rounded tops.

In addition to the cedars there were a few pines dotted here and there, slim tall-growing trees, their scanty limbs spaced wide apart, trees that had grown to maturity from thin roots that had found scant nourishment in the cracks of the stones through which they'd thrust.

"Vhy you stop now?" Viatsolof demanded.

"We was just looking around, trying to get our bearings," Longarm replied. "And wondering how we were going to get our horses down this here rock wall."

"Horses stay. Ve go," the Russian said curtly.

"Now, hold on!" Longarm protested. "Me and Charley both carry all our gear in our saddlebags. We can't just leave them and our rifles and saddles and horses up here! Anybody that was passing by and seen our stuff could steal everything we got if they took a notion to load it up and carry it off!"

Obviously, this was an idea which had not yet occurred to their captor. Viatsolof blinked, and a frown spread over his face. He was silent for a few moments, then he nodded and said, "Is close to here cave. You give me parole you do not run or shoot, and I show you it. Then you bring saddles. Horses no good vhere ve go."

Longarm and Hudson exchanged questioning glances. Then Hudson shrugged and said, "I don't guess we've got much choice, Longarm. But it's up to you. I only got one idea."

He raised his hand and shielded it from Viatsolof's eyes by holding it pressed to his body. Then he made a fist, leaving his forefinger extended, and crooked his middle finger as though he was pressing a trigger. At the same time he jerked his head almost imperceptibly toward the old Russian.

Longarm shook his head. "No, Charley," he said firmly. "You know just as well as I do that we ain't that kind."

"Sure. I knew what you'd say, but it was the only idea I could come up with."

"Anyways, I been doing some thinking," Longarm went on, "that Viatsolof ain't no spring chicken, and he don't have no horse. He had to've come here shank's mare from wherever he started, so it can't be real far."

93

"Now, that hadn't struck me before," Hudson admitted. "But you're right. If he could get here walking, we can sure as hell get to where he started from without a lot of trouble."

"That's how I figure it," Longarm said.

"Let's go ahead and cache our gear, then," Hudson said. "I'll get the horses up close as I can."

As Hudson started toward the horses, Longarm turned back to Viatsolof, who had already taken a step or two toward the canyon rim.

"All right," Longarm said. "We ain't going to give you no trouble. We'll cache our saddles and stuff here, but what about the horses?"

Viatsolof waved at the broad grassy expanse they'd just crossed. "Is here only place you leave them. Vhere ve go no grass is."

Looking back through the ragged stand of trees at the canyon edge, Longarm studied it for a moment, recalling that they'd seen no one on the way from the logging stand to where they were now, and nodded.

"I'd sure hate to be stuck out here, should something happen to 'em," he said. "But I guess we just got to take the risk."

Hudson came up, leading the horses, just as Longarm made his remark. He said, "You've been thinking along the same lines I was, I see. But I didn't get any further than you."

"Chewing over it won't cure things, either," Longarm told his companion. "All we can do is go with the old fellow and see if we can get along with whatever bunch he's tied into. Let's unload, then, soon as he shows us where the cache is."

Viatsolof had already started walking along the canyon's rim. He followed it for a short distance, ten or a dozen paces, moved to the very edge of the drop-off and dropped to his knees at a point where the dim trail veered around a deep vee in the canyon rim. He gestured to the vee.

"Is down here cave," he said over his shoulder.

"You mean it opens off of the canyon wall?" Longarm asked.

Viatsolof nodded. "Come. I show you steps to go down."

Before Longarm could start toward the canyon rim, Hudson put a restraining hand on his arm. Keeping his voice low, he said, "I don't like this one little bit, Longarm. That old fellow can see I can't do much of a job climbing. How in hell do we know what that old geezer's got up his sleeve?"

"So far his story's hung together," Longarm replied. "And I got to think about the job I was sent here to do for the Indian Bureau. Right now, it looks like he's about the best lead I've got to them. Which ain't to say I don't aim to keep my eyes open and mind my p's and q's."

"You think it's safe to do what he says?"

"Why, there ain't nothing that's always safe, Charley. But I tell you what. You take my rifle—I can't handle it if I got climbing to do. Then you back off a little ways and keep your eyes on things while I go down and look at that cave. If I hear you or him shoot, I can skin back up here in a jiffy."

"All right, if you say so. I hired on with you, so that makes you the boss. You go ahead, and I'll be ready to back you up if anything don't look right."

As Hudson turned back to the horses, Longarm stepped over to Viatsolof and said, "I'm as ready as I'll ever be. Just show me the place I need to start from."

Gesturing toward the vee in the canyon wall, the old man pointed downward. "Is close," he said. "Two or three steps, you find easy."

Longarm nodded and went to the apex of the vee. Bending forward, he could see edges of cracks and small jagged ledges that showed signs they'd been used as a ladder. Turning, he spread himself flat on his belly and pushed himself slowly down over the edge of the ledge.

Chapter 9

Although Longarm's position was precarious, the distance to the next safe foothold was not great. He had little difficulty in lowering himself to the narrow, roughly horizontal shelf almost a foot wide. The shelf curved around the mottled grey face of a smooth stone shoulder, and when he'd edged along it for a half dozen feet, Longarm saw the gaping black mouth of a cavern. He reached it in another three or four careful steps and discovered he could step inside without brushing the crown of his hat on the top arch.

Stopping just inside the opening to the low arch-topped recess, Longarm took a match from his vest pocket and scraped it across his iron-hard thumbnail. When the match flared into flame its light showed the gently curving walls of a cavern a dozen or so feet deep. Holding the burning match above his head, Longarm gave the enclosure a quick inspection.

Only a few flicking glances were needed to show him that there were no signs anyone had visited it recently.

When the match began to scorch his fingers he flicked it out and returned to the ledge. From there he eased his way back to the point where he'd descended.

Hudson's head appeared above him just as Longarm reached the notch in the cliff wall. He asked, "What'd you find?"

"Just like the old fellow told us, it's a cave. Our gear'll be safe there, at least till we can figure out a way to come back after it. Start lowering away whenever you're ready to go to work. But we'll hang on to our bedrolls—and our rifles, too."

For the next quarter hour or so Longarm and Hudson worked busily, Hudson lowering the saddle gear to be stowed away, Longarm placing them in the cavern. When he spread their saddle blankets over the heap that he'd built Longarm stepped back and looked at his handiwork.

"Well, old son," he muttered, lighting the first cigar he'd allowed himself since the job of caching began, "now all you got to do is hope nobody messes around in here till you've closed this case you're on and get ready to start back."

"Here is place ve go down to river," Viatsolof told Longarm and Hudson after the trio had walked along the rim of the river gorge for the better part of a mile. Pointing to a spot in the dimly marked rim trail a few paces ahead the old warrior went on, "Trail is begin there."

"I guess I can't make it out yet," Longarm told their captor after following his pointing finger with his eyes. He kept his voice mild.

"Is trail!" the Russian insisted. "You look good, you find it!"

"I guess it's like that crack in the wall where we left our gear," Longarm replied. "You're the one that knows the country, not us. Suppose you go first this time."

"You have give parole," Viatsolof reminded him. "Still my prisoners you are. Come. I veel be close in back."

Slowly and cautiously, keeping his distance from Longarm and Hudson, the old man watched while the two edged along the trail until it widened. Then he lifted the muzzle of his rifle and indicated a spot where a crevice began at the side of the trail.

Longarm looked at the wide crack in the sheer stone belt that ran along the rim. He said, "That ain't no better than the place where we left our gear. It sure ain't what I'd call a trail, and you can see my friend here's just got one good leg. I'd feel a mite better if I just looked along it a ways before we start out."

"Go to look, then!" Viatsolof told him. "You veel find I am not lie to you."

Moving up to the brink of the canyon, Longarm leaned forward. Only then did he see that the crack widened into a ledge just below the lip of the canyon rim. Although it was narrow and steep where it first appeared, a short distance away it widened. A horse could not have used it, but the ledge would easily accommodate men walking in single file, and the slant was not too great for Hudson to handle.

He shifted his attention to the lower section. Although he could not follow the full course of the ledge with his eyes, Longarm could tell that the canyon into which it led was both wide and deep and that as it curved in its gentle sweep it also slanted downward. From his vantage point there was only a short stretch of the canyon floor visible, but he could see the glinting water of the river that spanned most of the width of the bottom of the vast stone split.

Longarm inched backward along the ledge until he reached a place where the narow shelf was wide enough to allow him to turn around. Facing his destination now, he could move faster. A few minutes' steady progress brought

99

him back to the point where Hudson and Viatsolof were waiting.

Viatsolof looked at Longarm, his eyes in their puffed pouched sockets holding a question. When Longarm did not volunteer any information, the Russian said, "You see I am say truth to you, nyet?"

"I never called you a liar," Longarm said. "I just wanted to make sure."

"If you're satisfied I can handle going down, that's all I need to know," Hudson put in. "And if we're going to get to wherever it is he's taking us, we better be moving on."

"Go, then," the old Russian urged. "I am to follow last."

With Longarm leading, the three began edging along the narrow ledge. They reached the point where Longarm had turned back and pushed on at a bit quicker pace as the ledge widened steadily to the point where they could move normally. The ledge became a shelf, and Hudson moved up to walk beside Longarm.

"You figure we're getting anyplace, or is this just a wild-goose chase?" he asked.

"Oh, I'm sure now that the old fellow ain't been lying to us. Once we get to wherever it is that his people are camped, half of our job's going to be done. Redskins are the same everyplace I know about. One tribe knows all there is to know about the others, and it ain't going to be much of a trick for us to find out what the trouble is that's stirring things up between them and the loggers."

"And what happens when you do?"

"That's a hill I ain't aiming to climb up till I get to it. All I know is that I got to stop a war before it starts, and that's what I'm aiming to do, regardless of what it takes or whoever tries to stop me."

• • •

100

For what seemed a very long time, Longarm and Hudson and Viatsolof had been walking steadily, making their way upriver beside the shallow water of the river to which a little creek had led them from the end of the narrow trail. The sun had moved to slant westward by the time they'd set out, and now with its glare gone from most of the river's surface they could get a better idea of its character.

Though the river was broad, it was actually carrying little more water than would a creek. In some places where a jutting rise along the bank created shadows Longarm could see just how shallow the water was. Except for a few deep holes in the river bottom, only a few inches of water were flowing over the rocks and small boulders of its bed. Everywhere Longarm looked the water had a greenish-brown tinge, and long yellowish streaks of foam floated on its surface.

Along the river's bank a strip of dark sandy soil offered an easier passage than could be seen in the boulder-strewn stretch between the river and the high walls of the canyon through which it flowed. In the deeper stretches of the river the current roiled ominously in circling eddies and the water looked dark and foreboding. However, where the bottom shoaled into shallows the hue of the water lightened and an almost musical humming rose from the current.

On both sides of the riverbed high striated bluffs rose to define the channel the water had formed when it was in flood and rushing in its progress to the sea. Between the sandy strip at the water's edge and the base of the cliffs where the trail ran, broad expanses of stones lined the ground. The smallest were the size of a man's fist, the biggest were as large as prairie schooners.

Beyond the crestline of the bluffs tall trees towered. Longarm turned to Charley Hudson and asked, "Now, what

101

kind of trees would them be up ahead? Unless they're a lot farther away than I figure they are, they ain't big enough to be redwoods."

"They are, though," Hudson answered. "But they're not the same kind of redwood we passed through on the way up here. They don't grow as tall and the trunks aren't as big around."

"And I guess where there's trees, there's loggers?"

"Oh, there's a few left hereabouts," Hudson said. "But most of them moved farther south a long time ago. The trees, well, you saw the stands down in the country around Humboldt Bay. You know how big they grow down there, Longarm. It's almost as easy to handle the big trees as it is the kind you'll find up here farther to the north, and they cut up into a lot more boards for the same amount of work that a crew'd put in on one up here."

"Them trees won't get much bigger, then?"

"No. But I've seen some of the smaller redwoods to the north of here, along the bend of the Smith River. And I know there are still some logging stands even farther upriver, where the land's not so broken up and it's easier to work."

"But you've never been along here, where we are now?"

Hudson shook his head. "I'm just remembering what I've seen on maps and heard some of the woods drifters talking about."

"Then you don't rightly know just exactly where we are, either? Or where we might be heading?"

"No, of course not. But it seems to me like we've been walking long enough to get to wherever it is we're going."

"Let's see what the old fellow says about it."

Stepping away from the hint of a path that bordered the river, Longarm turned to call to Viatsolof, who had been maintaining his usual position behind Longarm and Hudson.

"How much farther we got to go?" Longarm called. "We've been going shank's mare a long ways, and my feet're starting to tell me they'd just as soon have me off of 'em."

"Not much," the old man replied. "People just a little bit more far, now." He pointed ahead and went on, "To vhere is bend."

Longarm turned to follow his gesture and saw that perhaps a quarter of a mile ahead the river swept in a wide curve. The terrain beyond it was invisible behind the tall bluff of the bank. He turned back long enough to nod in acknowledgment, then caught up with Hudson, who had kept moving steadily.

"Looks like we're finally going to get there," he told Hudson. "And I'd sure be glad not to have to take more'n a few more steps. I guess I been forking a horse such a long time that my feet ain't used to doing all the work I've been puttin' on them."

They plodded on toward the high bluff that marked the river's bend and reached its base. Now they could see for the first time that a wide stretch of rippling water spread across the entire floor of the canyon, backed up behind a broad line of jutting branches and twigs and short expanses of humped sandy stretches that spanned the river at the mouth of the broad canyon beyond.

"Slash and trash!" Hudson snorted. "Logger's trash! They've closed the river just as solid as if they'd built a dam across it here!"

"It looks to me like that's what they did," Longarm said. "Except that it just don't stand to reason they'd want to close down the river."

"It would if they're logging upriver from here," Hudson pointed out. "But unless some outlaw outfit's opening up a new stand upriver, I can't see why they'd—" He broke off, shaking his head. "No, Longarm. That's not what it looks like down there. It's not like a dam a logging crew'd build. For one thing, there's not any key logs in it."

"Now, what's a key log?" Longarm asked.

"When a logging crew builds a dam like that to use for a gathering pond, they put up a stretch of big logs across the river in the middle and lash 'em down with cables," Hudson explained. "Then when they get ready to float the logs downriver, they chop the cables and let the logs float downriver behind the head the water raises."

While they talked they'd been moving steadily. Beyond them now they could see a solid sheet of water, its wind-rippled surface looking like a small lake that reached from the base of the cliff where they stood to another sheer rock wall on the opposite side of the river. As they started around the bulge at the base of the tall curved formation and saw what lay ahead of them, Longarm frowned.

"We ain't going to push ahead much farther unless we swim or wade," he said as he turned back to Hudson. "It don't look like there's enough room for a trail between the river and that big bluff on this side of the river."

Hudson's eyes had also been fixed on the terrain in front of them. He said, "There's bound to be, Longarm. We're still too far away to see it, that's all."

As though he'd been able to hear the exchange between them, Viatsolof called, "Is vide enough to go on! Not to stop here! Move! And to canyon vall stay close!"

Acknowledging the shout with a wave, Longarm continued his slow careful progress. The trail continued to diminish in width until there was barely room for him and Hudson to walk in single file along the few inches of sandy earth that spanned the space between the rock wall and the water. Their boots sank almost an inch each time they took a forward step, and when they lifted their feet water seeped into the deep prints left on the soggy sandy soil and filled them almost at once.

During their slow progress the sun had been dropping steadily behind the canyon rim. The line of sunshine had crept across the water's surface, and in the dark shadowed strip of the glass-clear water each hump and stone and shadow on the river bottom could be seen clearly. Longarm's eyes caught a flash of silver. He looked more closely at the gleaming spot and saw a large fish lying on its side in the shallows. He gazed at it for a moment watching its feeble efforts to right itself, then called to his companion.

"Come take a look, Charley! There's a damn big fish in the river here that looks like it's sick or something!"

Hudson moved to Longarm's side, gazed at the fish for a moment and nodded. He said, "Steelhead spawner. Couldn't get through the brush and stuff that's damming up the river and go back to the ocean."

"You better tell me again, this time so I can understand what you're talking about."

"Well, there's two kinds of fish in all these rivers. One's steelhead and the other's salmon," Hudson explained. "Both of them live part of the time in the ocean and come up the rivers to lay their eggs. Then they go back to salt water and stay in the ocean for a while, but they swim back up the river again the next year at spawning time."

"And they do that over and over every year?"

"Steelhead do, they don't die after they've spawned. The salmon generally die after they've dropped their eggs. Of course when the fish are moving a lot, that's when the redskins get busy and spear'em. If you'll recall, I mentioned that to you when we were talking about the trouble between them and the loggers."

"I guess I didn't catch on," Longarm replied. "I know the Indians out in this country here depend on fish a lot, that's why they're on the outs with the timber people for getting the rivers all messed up. But there's a whole hell of a lot that I dont' know about fish."

"Well, now you know a little bit more than you did before." Hudson smiled. "I just didn't know that you hadn't—" He broke off as a shout came from Viatsolof.

"Not to stop!" the old man called. "Stay close to cliff! Not try to get avay in river or I shoot you!"

"Don't worry, we ain't trying no funny stuff!" Longarm shouted in reply. He turned back to Hudson and went on, "We better not rile the old fellow. If he gets mad, he might take a notion to shoot one of us, and I wouldn't be surprised if he's pretty good with that old gun he's toting."

"He'd have to be, just to stay alive this long in such wild country," Hudson agreed. "But for all the moving along we've been doing, we don't seem to be getting any closer to where he's taking us."

They had walked the short distance back to the trail at the foot of the high cliff while they talked. Viatsolof was waiting for them, though he was careful to keep at a distance. He made a gesture toward the trail ahead. Both men turned onto it and started upriver again. Here through the shallow water they could see more dead or dying fish lying on the bottom, and after they'd covered a short distance the fitful breeze from upriver brought an unpleasant odor to their noses.

"Smells to me like there's something big dead not too far from here," Longarm said.

"I'd imagine it's a deer carcass," Hudson said, "or maybe a bear."

"Well, I'll be glad when we get on past it," Longarm said. "Whatever it is, it's sure making a big stink. Let's speed up a little bit and get on past it quick as we can."

Though the narrow trail between the high wall of the cliff and the riverbed made fast progress difficult, Longarm and Hudson increased their pace. The recurring bends in the high cliff's walls made really fast progress difficult and they'd kept to their speedier walk for only a hundred yards or so when a shout from Viatsolof sounded behind them.

"Slow!" he yelled. "You run more, I shoot!"

Longarm glanced behind them. Viatsolof had just rounded one of the many curves in the cliff that bordered the riverbank. He was shouldering his ancient rifle when Longarm saw him.

"Hit the dirt!" Longarm called over his shoulder to Hudson as he dropped flat on the narrow path.

Hudson reacted just in time and dropped to the ground at once. The deep booming bark of the old Russian's rifle broke the stillness. Its slug whistled over Hudson's prone form and splatted into the stone side of the high cliff that bordered the river.

"Don't shoot again!" Hudson yelled. "We're not trying to get away!"

Longarm had begun to lever himself to his feet when Hudson called out. He looked back at Viatsolof. The old warrior had not sought cover. He was standing on the narrow path beside the river reloading his ancient weapon. Longarm brought up his Winchester in the automatic reaction to danger that many narrow escapes had caused to become instinctive. His finger closed on the trigger and he was beginning to squeeze off his shot when a woman's voice from the riverbank ahead of them broke the silence.

"No!" she cried. "Not to shoot! Please! Let my father live and I promise that he will not harm you!"

Chapter 10

Longarm eased the pressure of his trigger finger and lifted his head as he turned to look for the woman who'd spoken. She was standing in the trail a short distance behind them and her broad face was still twisted in the agony of pleading that had been carried in the worried tone of her voice.

"I ain't hankering to kill anybody, ma'am," he assured her. "But if that old fellow shooting at us from over yonder lets off one more round at me and my friend, he might persuade me to change my mind."

"Just don't hurt him," the woman said quickly. "I'm sure I can stop him from doing any more shooting at either of you."

Turning, she raised her voice and started speaking in one of the Indian tongues that was strange to Longarm. She said only a few words, but at the first sound of her voice Viatsolof lowered his rifle. He did not answer her, but shifted the muzzle of the ancient weapon until it was pointing at the ground. Then he started moving toward her and Longarm.

Longarm had been studying the newcomer while her attention was concentrated on Viatsolof. She was not a girl, but a young woman totally matured, though when Longarm tried to guess her age he found himself totally baffled. She could have been a mature twenty or a youthful thirty or forty.

Like most northern coast Indians, her hair was coarse and jet-black, drawn into a loose fall that framed her face and fell over her shoulders. Her face was a broadened oval and her eyes closer to being oval than round. Her nose was small and slightly flattened, her lips full, and her jaw rounded but firm. She had on a calico dress that dropped from her shoulders in a straight line to mid-calf and effectively concealed her figure.

"You say that man's your father?" Longarm asked as she turned back to him.

Nodding, she answered, "Yes. And you can see that he's old and gets excited easily. He's not a killer."

"I've already got acquainted with him," Longarm told her. "And you might be right about him not being a killer, but that didn't stop him from taking a shot or two at me and my friend here when we first ran into him."

"He didn't hit you, I can see that."

"If saying so don't hurt your feelings none, he ain't a real sure shot," Longarm said. "And that old rifle he's got don't carry none too true."

"I'm glad he missed!" she breathed. "I suppose you kept him talking and finally agreed to come here with him?"

"That wasn't no trouble after we got him to parlay with us," Longarm told her. "Then when we found out a little bit more, we figured it wasn't going to hurt us a bit to come along with him. Matter of fact, we were heading this way to see if we could find you folks."

110

"You know who my father is, then?" she asked.

"We know the name he gave us when we first ran into him, but that's the size of it," Longarm answered.

"I'd imagine that he gave you his Russian name and not his Indian one," she said. "Our people call him Korakoro. And my name is Klalish."

"I'm Custis Long," Longarm replied. "Deputy United States marshal. This fellow here is Charley Hudson, he's helping me do the job I was sent up here for."

Hudson has been silent, listening to the exchange between Longarm and the Indian girl. Now he put in, "And we know your father thinks he's still a soldier in the Russian army, even if there haven't been any Russian soldiers here for fifty years."

"Please, you'll have to forgive him!" Klalish exclaimed. "And me, too. I suppose I'm partly to blame for not going with him when he left the village early this morning. I didn't look for him back at any special time, but when the sun began to go down, I came to look for him. He goes out to scout the river trail every day, and I was sure I could find him."

"All by yourself?" Hudson frowned.

"Of course. I know my father's ways. I've had to look for him before when he's gone out as he did today."

"Is the town where you and him live close around here?" Longarm asked. "Because if it is, it sure don't show on none of the maps I've looked at. They don't show a single town that's anyplace in spitting distance."

"I can understand that," she said. "There aren't any white men's towns close by, and we move from one of our settlements to another—" She stopped, frowned, and went on, "I don't quite know how to explain it so everything will make sense to you."

"You're doing pretty good, so far," Longarm assured her. "Just keep on going."

"Well, there's not much difference between our tribe and the others close by. We are Hoopas, river Indians. Surely you know that we do not fight your people like the Cheyenne do, and the Sioux, and the other warrior tribes that live on the land farther from the ocean."

"To tell you the downright facts, I know a lot more about them other tribes than I do about your folks."

"We live like most of the tribes do here in this part of the country. We do not make war, now that all the Karanakas are gone. Our people move from one river to another during the times the fish runs are best. The salmon we take when they come into the rivers are our main food. We dry them and keep them to eat through the winter, when the fish have gone back to the ocean. Our people—" Klalish broke off as Viatsolof came up to them and stopped a pace or so away.

He was panting from the exertion of hurrying to reach them. He did not carry his ancient rifle at the ready now, but held it by the barrel and used it as a walking staff. Longarm and Klalish did not try to continue their conversation, but waited for the old man to speak.

Viatsolof said nothing until his gasping breathing settled down. When he did speak he did not shout, but loosed a string of words that sounded to Longarm like nothing but gibberish. When the old soldier finally stopped talking, Klalish replied in the same strangely liquid tongue. Their conversation lasted only a few moments, then she turned back to Longarm.

"There is a thing Father said that I do not understand," she said. The tone of her voice as well as her worried frown showed her puzzlement. "Why did he tell me that you are his prisoners?"

"Oh, he told us the same thing," Longarm replied. "And we didn't feel like arguing. All we'd've done was to make him mad. I figured real quick that the easiest way for us to get where we wanted to go was to give in and just let him take us along. Turns out that was the best thing we could've done, because here we are."

"A moment ago you said that you're a United States marshal," Klalish sad. "Have you come here to arrest some of our people?"

"It ain't exactly like that," Longarm answered. He stopped to think for a moment, then went on, "It's sorta mixed up, but maybe I can get it all sorted out for you. Like I said, it was the Indian Bureau that sent me out looking for your tribe."

"But the Indian agent was here only a month or so ago," Klalish said. "He said nothing about us having done anything wrong. Did he find that our people have broken some laws and send you here to arrest us?"

"Even if I'm a United States marshal, I ain't here to arrest nobody," Longarm assured her. "Not right now, anyways. What I've come here to do is—" He stopped again, searching for the right words to describe his mission. Shaking his head, he said, "The Indian Bureau got word that there's trouble brewing between your folks and the loggers who're cutting down the redwood trees."

"If the Indian Bureau sent you, does that mean you're on our side and you didn't come here to help the tree cutters?"

Before Longarm could reply, Viatsolof broke in. He began talking at once, ignoring Longarm and Hudson, addressing himself to Klalish in their own soft unaccented tongue. He talked for what seemed to be a long time while she listened intently. At last she turned back to Longarm.

"My father is confused," she explained. "He's sure you are here to find more of the big trees for the loggers to cut down, but they have already sent men up here to look, and they found what we already knew. Few of the big, big trees grow north of this river here."

113

"Maybe you better tell him the real reason, then," Longarm suggested. "What I'm here for is to keep everything peaceful."

Klalish stood silently thoughtful for a moment, then she nodded and said, "I understand that, Marshal Long. But how can you do that? You are one man, and there are many of the men who cut our trees and spoil our rivers. When you were on the way to where we are now, you must have seen what the last tree cutters who were here did to this river."

"You mean that stinking stretch downriver from here? Where the river widens out just a little ways back?" Longarm asked.

"Yes."

"Oh, I saw it, all right. And smelled it, too."

"From what you're asking me, I'm sure you saw the dead fish and all the rest?"

Longarm nodded. "Maybe we didn't see all of it, but just from the little looking around we had time to do I'd say it sure wasn't what you'd call something to be proud of."

"That is the fault of the men who cut the trees," she said. "They stop the running of the rivers, too, when they make ponds to keep their logs in. The fish who come up to lay their eggs are caught by the dams and cannot go back to the sea. They die behind the dams."

"So that's why all them dead fish are laying on the bottom of the river," Longarm said.

"It is not the first of such places," Klalish said. Longarm could sense that she was suppressing the anger she felt as she went on, "And it will not be the last, if the tree cutters come back. This is our land, Marshal Long! We share it with other tribes, but we do not spoil it for your people. Why do your people spoil our land for us?"

"This ain't the time or place to talk about that," Longarm told her. "Later on, when me and my friend here learn the lay of the land and find out a little bit about what's going on, maybe you can tell me some more. But now that we've found out we're at the place we started for, we need somewhere to settle down in and rest for a little spell. We've been traveling over some pretty rough country."

Viatsolof had been standing beside Klalish, looking from her to Longarm and back at her again during their long exchange. Now he broke in to say something to Klalish in the strange tongue they shared. After a moment she nodded and turned back to Longarm and Hudson.

"My father understands better now that you and your friend are not here to harm us," she said. "He wants you to come with us to our village and rest from your long trip."

"Well, now, that's right thoughtful," Longarm replied. "But we still have to go talk to the other tribes that live along these rivers. We'll be glad to stay the night, and maybe have him tell us whereabouts we can find them other Indians, where they're living and all like that, but once we know where to head for, we'll have to be pushing on."

"I have not told you all there is," Klalish said. "All the headmen of the large tribes of our people are coming here soon. For many months they have talked about the tree cutting men, and how they are ruining our rivers. And one of the tribes was attacked. Now, they want to see what we can do to stop them from doing this."

"Hold on a minute!" Longarm frowned. "If your friends are figuring to take on the loggers, what it sounds like to me is that there's a fight getting stirred up!"

"Like Captain Jack and his bunch!" Hudson put in. "It wasn't too long ago, ten years or so as I remember, that the Modocs over to the west in the lava beds country got crossways with the settlers and had a pretty good sized war going before things settled down."

"We Hoopas are not like the Modocs," Klalish said. Her voice was suddenly cold. "Our people are civilized, even if we do hold to our own old ways." Turning away from Hudson, she said to Longarm, "But if you have really come here to help us, this is your chance to talk to the headmen, and you will not have to travel to find them."

"You're sure they'll all be here?"

Klalish shook her head. "Nobody could be sure of that, Marshal Long. We have asked all of them—"

"Excuse me for busting in on you, but maybe you won't mind telling me just who you mean when you say all of them," Longarm suggested.

"Of course, I can't be sure all of the tribes we've sent a message to will be here," she said. "But we've sent word to the few Hoopa people who're left down by the big bay, and then there are the Chelulas, Tolowas, Umpquahs, Yukis, Klamaths, Pomos, Karoks and Yuroks. To the east there are Chimarikos, but we have little to do with them, they are still savages. There are some Wintus left and a few Modocs who came here to resettle after they lost their big fight, and we've invited them, too. Of course, we don't know how many will be here."

"It sounds to me like you oughta have a crowd," Longarm said. "I didn't know there was all that many kinds of Indians around here."

"Some of the tribes are small," Klalish said. "And some might not show up. But I think most of them will. You see, we Hoopas live at peace with everyone, even with your people, when you allow us to."

"Now, you shouldn't feel like all of us are down on you, just because you've had trouble with a few loggers!" Longarm said.

"Of course not!" Klalish exclaimed. "And we're certainly not trying to stir up trouble. We hope we can stop trouble from starting."

"Well, when you put it that way, it makes a lot of sense. I'll just take up your daddy's invite."

"That will please him," she said.

"We'll call everything settled for right now," Longarm told her. "I guess there'll be someplace where we're going for us to spread our bedrolls?"

"Don't worry," Klalish assured him. "Our people will make you welcome."

"We might as well go along with you and him, then," Longarm suggested. "You lead on. Me and Charley'll be right behind you."

Sunset's red was tinging the sky behind them when Longarm and Hudson looked beyond Viatsolof and Klalish and saw the scattered array of small huts that were spaced willy-nilly in cleared spots among the trees.

A few of the dwellings had been made from thick slabs of bark, and their outlines were canted and irregular, but even in the shadows that held sway below the towering branches of the big trees that made up the grove, Longarm could see that most of the dwellings had been built by digging trenches to form a rough square or rectangle and burying wide planks from the big trees upright in them, then adding a slanted shed roof.

All the structures were small, and none of them that he saw had windows. Slabs of wood or bark hung on rawhide thongs above rounded doorways, closing the only openings that any of the houses offered. Small rock-ringed fires burned near many of the two or three dozen of the little dwellings, but the others seemed to be deserted.

"I just wonder how many people can crowd into one of those little shanties," Hudson remarked to Longarm as the details of the settlement became visible. "And what they're bound to smell like inside."

"There ain't one of them that wouldn't hold a half dozen or so," Longarm estimated. "Except it sure don't look like there's people in many of 'em."

"Maybe we'll find out," Hudson went on, jerking his head toward Klalish, who'd been walking ahead of them beside her father. She had left him and was coming toward them.

"You must find yourself a house before it is dark," she said. "You will know which ones are empty. This is the time when we have supper, and there will be fires at those where our people are living." She pointed to one of the little huts. "That is where Father and I live. As soon as I can go in and build a fire, I will cook food for our supper."

"Are you sure you can spare any food?" Longarm asked.

"We have more than enough for our own needs, and the men who are away fishing now will bring fish back with them. When we saw the river here would not have any, they went to the next one close by."

"So that's why there's so many houses that ain't got folks living in 'em," Longarm said. "I was sorta wondering."

"We will need all the houses when our own men come back and when the other tribes arrive," Klalish said. "And we will need the fish our men will return with. But I am sure there will be enough for everyone."

"It looks to me like we got here just when we might be able to do the most good," Longarm observed. "But I reckon your people've been planning on this shindy for quite a while."

"We have talked among our own people for many moons," she agreed. "And to some from the other tribes.

118

But this will be the first time that all the tribes will be here—if all of them take our invitation, that is."

"If you don't mind me saying so, Klalish, you talk like you had a lot of schooling," Hudson put in.

"I have been to Indian School. But there will be time later to talk of such things," she said. "I must go and attend to my father now. Choose your house, and when you are ready, come and have supper with Father and me. When you have shared a meal, you will no longer be enemies, but friends."

Longarm turned to Hudson after Klalish had gone and said, "Unless you got some other idea, we might just as well settle down in this house in front of us. It don't look like there's anybody living in it, there ain't no fire in front of the door."

He walked over to the circle of bark that hung on the wall facing them and pulled it aside. An opening as round as the piece of bark but a bit smaller in diameter had been cut in the wide planks forming the wall. Beyond the opening the interior was blacker than a moonless midnight sky.

"Well," he went on, "you might as well go in first while I hold the door open."

Hudson stepped up to the dark circular opening and stuck his head and shoulders inside. A moment later he pulled his head out, and said, "I think I'd rather sleep under one of these trees than be shut up in a place like that, Longarm! It'd give me the willies all night! Besides, it stinks just like an outhouse inside there."

Longarm moved to the yawning hole and leaned forward. The smell was not as bad as he'd expected it to be from Hudson's remark, but even his keen eyes could not penetrate the darkness that shrouded the interior. He fished a match from his pocket and flicked his thumbnail across it. Blinking his eyes to peer through the darkness he could see that there was no furniture, not even a stove, in the house.

He also saw something else. One of the boards of the floor had been removed and at once his nose identified the gap as being the source of the odor to which Hudson had objected. He backed out of the circular doorway, and turned to his companion.

"I think we did pick us an outhouse by mistake," Longarm said. "Let's see if we can't do better." He looked around at the other small huts in the grove. Dim gleams of light shone around the edges of the bark slabs that closed the entry to the nearest. A dozen paces away, there was a hut from which no light escaped. He went on, "I don't guess it makes much never-mind whichever one we pick out, long as nobody's living in it, and it don't look like there's anybody in that one over yonder."

They walked over to the hut and Longarm held the bark slab of the entry aside while Hudson looked in. When he turned away he said, "This one don't stink too bad. I guess it's all right, if you want to stay in it, but to tell you the truth, I'd rather sleep outside of one of these shanties than in it."

"We can always move to another one if this one smells bad," Longarm suggested.

"What I need right now is some grub," Hudson said. "We'll settle down for the night later on. Right now I'm so hungry I could eat a raw steak without even putting salt on it."

Longarm had taken one of his long thin cigars from his pocket while Hudson was speaking. He lighted it, and spoke through the cloud of smoke from his first deep inhalation.

"I feel just about like you do," he agreed. "But that don't bother me as much as thinking about what we got to do when all them Indians get here. I've been in a few scrapes, but nothing that'll hold up to this. I got to figure out how to make aces outa deuces. Because if I don't play my cards right when all them redskins get together, they're going to start a war, and I'm going to be the one that'll be blamed for it!"

Chapter 11

"I got to say one thing," Longarm told Klalish as he wiped his lips with a flourish of his bandana. "I ain't much of a fish eater. It's pretty generally just like chicken, you eat and eat and even when you know your belly's full it still feels like your throat's been cut. But that smoked salmon you dished up for our supper was real tasty. It was good as any beefsteak I ever put away."

"I'll join up with you in that," Hudson agreed. "It's the best fish I've ever tasted."

Longarm, Hudson and Klalish were sitting beside a dying fire outside of the little house occupied by her and her father. Alexis Viatsolof had left them only a few moments earlier. He'd wolfed down a sizeable portion of the smoked salmon without speaking, then stood up abruptly to tell them that he was sleepy and was going to bed. Viatsolof's brief announcement ended, he'd pulled the bark door aside, and stepped into the cabin.

"You are kind to tell me," Klalish said. "But you might

not say the same thing near the end of winter, after smoked fish is all you have eaten for three or four months. Wait until the men come back. They will bring fresh fish with them, and that will be even better."

"I still say it was good," Longarm said through the veil of smoke from the cigar he'd lighted. "The only thing I'm sorry about is that your daddy went to bed so soon."

"He had more sense than us," Charley Hudson put in. "And I can take a hint as quick as the next one. I'm about as tired as I can ever remember being. I'm going to go to bed myself."

"You go ahead, then," Longarm told him. "I was figuring on asking the old fellow about this big powwow tomorrow." He turned to Klalish and went on, "Maybe you'll tell me, instead of him?"

"Of course," she offered. "I suppose I know about as well as Father what our people are trying to get done."

"Then I'll shove off," Hudson said. He smothered a yawn as he stood up and went on, "Just don't make too much noise when you come in, Longarm. It looks like we've got some busy days coming up, and I'm way behind on sleep."

"I'll be along presently," Longarm told him. "And I'll sleep a lot sounder if I got some idea of what's ahead of us."

"Father would've told you, I'm sure," Klalish said as she and Longarm watched Hudson disappear into the darkness. Before he'd taken more than three or four steps from the faint glow of the dying fire's last embers he had disappeared in the inky blackness beyond the small blaze.

"About all I know of what's going on is that your daddy's got some kind of confabulation fixed up," Longarm said as he turned back to Klalish.

"I suppose you'd call it a council," she said. "The men who cut down the redwood trees have been exploring around here, not once, but three or four times. Father's sure—and so am I—that they look for places where there are trees to cut down."

"But they haven't cut any?"

"No. Some do not stop, but only pass by in their boats as they go up the river. Some have gone as far as the lands of the Chimarikos and the Wintus, but none I have heard about have stayed long."

"And you're sure none of 'em have stopped along here?"

"Yes. There was a time when they did, but now they only go by our lands."

"What about the other tribes that live up this way? Have these fellows been prowling around their reservations?"

"There was a time when they did, but none have stopped to look lately."

"I guess your friends in other tribes would've told you if there'd been any up and down the coast, here?"

"Of course. I have talked to all our people along the ocean shore. The Pomos and Karoks and Chelulas and Yukis and Umpquahs and Klamaths and Tolowas and Yuroks and Hoopas."

"These Chimarikos and Wintus, are they coming to your shindy along with the others?"

"Yes. Either Father or I have taken word to them."

"Then maybe we can find out more about all this tomorrow morning. I guess he'll be around, too?"

Klalish nodded. "Of course. It was only that he was very tired that he went to bed so soon tonight. I could see that earlier, when we met by the river. I am glad that he did not stay up." A frown was flitting over her face as she spoke. "As our people say of the elders, he is carrying many years on his back."

"I figured he'd have to be," Longarm said. "It's been more than forty years since the Russians pulled out and went back home, and he'd've had to be a grown-up man when he first came here with their soldiers. How come he didn't go with the others when they gave up at Fort Ross and went back to Russia?"

Klalish shook her head and said, "He will not talk of his time with the Russians, not even to me."

"Well, my guess is that he was in some kinda trouble and just deserted from the Russian army, maybe even quite a while before they went back home."

"You may be right," she said. "All I know is that he had been with our people for many years before I was born," Klalish said thoughtfully. "And I have learned that even then they spoke of him as an old man."

"What about you?" Longarm asked. "How'd he come to tie up with your mother?"

"Of that, I know only bits and pieces that the elders have spoken of. My mother died giving birth to me, but instead of following our tribe's custom of giving me to another family, Father put me with a woman who had a newborn child. When I was old enough he began caring for me himself and later he insisted that I go to Indian School. Very few women of our people have that chance."

"I was wondering where you learned to talk English so good."

"English is just about all I have left of my Indian School training. Except for that, I follow our tribe's old ways."

"You come by 'em rightfully, I guess."

"They are the ways our old people taught us, the ways they learned when they were growng up," Klalish said. "But I know it is not like your people do. You must always make new ways."

"Well, I don't see nothing wrong with either one," Longarm told her. "I don't do things like my daddy did because someplace along the line somebody came up with something better. But most of the time, I get orders from my boss that I've got to follow, just like he does when his boss tells him to do something."

"But that is when you are at work," she pointed out. "You must have time to do things that you wish to do yourself."

Longarm read the meaning behind Klalish's remarks. After a moment he said, "I don't guess I see what you're driving at. Maybe you better just come out flat-footed and tell me."

"Do I really need to do that?"

There was a smile in Klalish's voice. Even though they'd been talking for only a few minutes the coals of their supper fire had died to a few isolated red embers. All that Longarm could now see of her face was an occasional faint glinting from her eyes.

"No, I don't reckon you do," he said.

A soft rustle of Klalish's deerskin dress told Longarm that she was getting to her feet, then he could see her in vague outline against the long streaks of star-filled sky that were visible through the tree trunks.

"There are plenty of houses close by that have no one in them," she told him. "Come with me."

Longarm followed her without questioning. Klalish led him past two or three of the silent dark little houses. Enough starshine filtered through the branches and between the tree trunks for him to recognize the one in which he and Hudson were staying, but only because his bedroll was still leaning against the wall beside the door. A moment later, Klalish stopped beside another of the dwellings.

"There's no one using this house now," she said as she pushed aside the bark slab that covered its round doorway and gestured for him to enter.

"If you'll just stand where you are for a minute so I don't go to the wrong place when I come back, I'll step over to the cabin me and Hudson's in and get my bedroll," he offered. "We'll be a lot more comfortable on it than on the bare floor."

"Your idea is good," she agreed. "Go ahead."

A half dozen long steps took Longarm back to his own cabin, and in a moment he returned to find Klalish still standing at the door of the cabin she'd selected.

"Go on in," she told him. "I can handle the door easier than you would."

Longarm put one of his long legs through the round black hole of the door opening and levered himself through it. The interior of the little shanty was pitch-black, the circular door hole defined by the lighter darkness of the starry night. Even that bit of light disappeared almost at once, for while he was shaking the folds from his bedroll and spreading it on the floor Klalish let the bark door slab swing back into place.

"I hope you don't mind being in the dark," she said.

Her voice was muffled for a moment and Longarm realized that its changed timbre was caused by the deerskin dress passing her lips as she took it off. Even though he could not be sure of what his ears were telling him, he wasted no time levering out of his boots and shedding his vest.

He was unbuckling his gun belt when he sensed the warmth of Klalish's body and felt her hand groping for him, then her fingers danced softly across his shoulders. He dropped the heavy gun belt and turned to stand facing her. His eyes had adjusted to the blackness now. In spite of the unlighted gloom of the one-room hut he could distinguish the outline of her body and the blurred dark shadows of her eyes and lips, the swell of her full breasts and their dark tips.

Oriented now, Klalish started to unbutton his shirt. Her warm fingers brushing his bare skin as she worked gave Longarm the beginning of an erection. He left to her the job of removing his shirt while he concentrated on freeing his long legs from his trousers.

Klalish had taken off the shirt by the time he'd stepped out of his trousers. She unbuttoned his long johns and was sliding them down his hips when her hands encountered the swelling at his groin. She let the underwear slip to the floor and began to caress his now-jutting shaft.

"You're a big man, Longarm," she said softly. "And I like big men. I think I will get much pleasure from being with you."

"If you don't, I reckon I'll be the first to know about it," he told her. "But if you want me to tell you the truth, I ain't a bit worried about us hitting it off."

Longarm was kicking his legs free of the clinging long johns as he spoke and now he turned back to Klalish. She had not released his swollen erection, but was fondling his shaft in her warm hands. She moved them up his sides now. Longarm bent his head to caress her bulging breasts with his lips, but Klalish had her hands on his rib cage now, and she sank down on the blanket, carrying him with her. After a moment of uncertain floundering after she'd pulled him down beside her, she rolled on to her back and once again sought his jutting shaft with her busily caressing fingers.

Longarm moved as readily as she did and slid between her thighs as she spread them. He felt her moist warmth engulfing him when she positioned him, and drove into her with a single lusty lunge that ended with a fleshly thwack as their bodies met in their merging.

Klalish loosed a long sigh that left her breathless when she first felt Longarm's full penetration. She embraced him doubly, bringing her legs high to lock them around his hips, her arms circling his broad chest and clasping behind his back. She began bucking almost at once when Longarm started to thrust steadily. He caught the quick irregular tempo of her movements and did his best to match them with his deep plunges.

Neither of them talked. After several moments of frenzy, Klalish's spastic and wildly uncontrolled jerks settled quickly into a steadier tempo. Her hips began to rise and fall in a twisting rhythmic response as she brought them up, timing her moves to meet Longarm's long measured downward lunges. Aside from an occasional joyous sigh that burst from Klalish's throat and now and then a gusty exhalation from Longam, the darkness was broken only by the soft thudding of their bodies coming together each time Longarm's swift and close-spaced drives ended with the collision of their hips.

Suddenly a small happy scream, only a bit louder than her whispered sighs, bubbled from Klalish's throat. She tightened her arms around Longarm's back and began rubbing her full-budded breasts against his chest's wiry curls. Longarm understood the sign. He stroked at a faster tempo. Klalish began trembling, and as Longarm steadily increased the speed of his drives and held himself pressed more firmly to her warm quivering body, Klalish's small cries grew louder and her spastic shudders took her at shorter intervals.

After a few more moments slid quickly past, Klalish began to arch her back and roll her hips from side to side. Longarm understood the new signals her quivering body was sending him and stroked faster. Klalish responded by gyrating her hips wildly. Her body was quivering constantly now and her small screams grew frantic, one following another until a steady column of sound was filling the cabin.

Longarm had been holding himself in firm control, and now let his feeling guide his thrusting and drove in triphammer lunges. A cry of climaxing ecstasy broke from Klalish's throat as she writhed and heaved in an uncontrollable final frenzy. Longarm freed his control and began jetting as Klalish loosed a final ululating cry that echoed through the small cabin. She passed her climax and lay as though her body was boneless while Longarm reached his own peak and fell forward on her warm still-quivering body.

Minute followed minute in the quietness of the midnight darkness inside the little cabin. Klalish was the first to break the stillness.

"I think I will not go back to my father's house tonight," she said. "Not if you can give me as much pleasure again."

"All I can do is try," Longarm told her. "But both of us have had a real busy day, and I got a hankering to catch a little shut-eye before we start up again. And sometime during the night we got some talking to do. I ain't been up in these parts before and there's a lot of questions I need answers to."

"Is this why you came here with me?"

"Now, you know better'n that, Klalish. Why, you're as pretty a girl as I ever saw before. I got to hankering after you the minute I saw you the first time."

"Then that is all I need to know," Klalish replied. "Let us sleep now. I will be ready if you awaken me again, or perhaps I will waken you. There will be time in the morning for us to talk of other things."

"That suits me to a tee," Longarm said. "Because right now all I can think about is getting some shut-eye."

Klalish was snuggling up to Longarm as he spoke. He pulled her close to him and stretched out beside her. In a few moments they were both sleeping soundly.

"I noticed you found someplace better than our cabin to bunk down in last night," Hudson told Longarm as the two men met a short distance away from Alexis Viatsolof's cabin.

131

Beyond the corner of the cabin Longarm could see Kla-lish bending over a small blaze, stirring a mixture of corn-meal and strips of dried salmon that bubbled in a big cast-iron cooking pot. Viatsolof was nowhere in sight.

Hudson went on, "Either that or you got up and started stirring around before I woke up this morning."

"Maybe it was a little bit of both," Longarm said. "What's important is that I've found out more'n we've dug up so far about what these redskin tribes up here are figuring to do."

"I got the idea yesterday they were getting ready to kick up their heels and start a ruckus."

"They still are," Longarm said. "Unless they change their minds after what goes on at the powwow they're sup-posed to have here today."

"Or unless you can change their minds for them?" Hud-son suggested.

"Maybe. I was sent up here to keep things peaceful be-tween the loggers and the Indians, and I still aim to do my job. But before I start trying to figure out how to go about it, I sure ain't going to get much of anyplace."

"You know who'd come off second best if these Indians begin jumping on the loggers."

"Sure. The thing I got to do is keep 'em from making that first jump. If this fuss gets that far, then someplace down the line all hell's gonna bust loose."

"Even if all the redskins from here on up to Canada show up, do you think there'll be enough of them to hold their own?" Hudson asked. "Some of the big camps here in the redwoods have as many as sixty or seventy men, not counting the skid teams and the dock-loading crews."

"Well, now," Longarm said, "what the Indians can do is gonna depend a lot on how many of 'em there is. And it'll depend a lot more on how many guns they can muster up, and what kind. I ain't seen many of 'em with what you'd call up-to-date rifles. Mostly they run to the kinda muzzle loaders old Viatsolof totes."

Hudson shook his head. "They won't get far when they match those old long-guns against the new Winchesters I've seen on most of the logging stands, to say nothing of the new Colt pistols."

Longarm nodded. "You're right about that. But I ain't aiming to let things go till it comes down to shooting."

"And what happens if you can't stop them?"

"I'll make up my mind about that later on, after I see how their powwow's shaping up," Longarm replied calmly. "I don't hold with jumping off of bridges till I come to 'em. But we better get ourselves some breakfast now. I'm hungry enough to start chewing on a poleaxed steer even before they drag him to the cooking fire."

Klalish looked up as Longarm came to stand beside her. "I got up and left before sunup," she said. "And I didn't want to rouse you. Father's already gone down to the river. He wanted to be there when the first of the other tribes gets here for the powwow."

"Well, soon as we put away a bite or two, we'll go have a look-see,"

"No. You got here just in time," Klalish said. "I was just cooking this for your breakfast—and for your friend's, too, of course. I've got to go find Father now. He's going to need my help if things go the way we hope they will."

"You run along, then," Longarm suggested. "Me and Charley can feed ourselves, and soon as we finish eating we'll be on down to give you a hand."

As Klalish moved away, Longarm stood watching her for a moment, then said to Hudson, "I guess we better hurry up and eat. Klalish ain't got all that much of an idea what she's going to be up against, trying to get a bunch of redskins from different tribes to do a job together."

"What gives you that idea?" Hudson asked.

"Because I've tried it myself a time or two, back in the Indian Nation and a few other places besides. What she's going to find is that none of them tribes is going to see things the same way. There's always two or three that'll see it all different. Then there'll be some that won't like either way, and I bet some wouldn't join up with another tribe to do anything, no matter what it is."

"What makes you so sure?" Hudson asked.

"Like I said a minute ago, back in the Indian Nation I've seen mixed-up bunches of redskins before. Maybe not any that's as different as all these, but pretty close to it."

"If you're right, we're just wasting our time, then."

"I ain't trying to throw no cold water on Klalish's idea," Longarm went on. "But her and old Viatsolof ain't got the chance of a snowball in hell to get this crowd to do anything the same way or at the same time. They'll be lucky if this powwow don't wind up with a big free-for-all."

Hudson frowned as he asked, "You think we'll get caught in the middle of it?"

"Oh, I wouldn't go that far. There's a chance I could be wrong, and anything that'll slow down them outlaw timber raiders is worth a try. Stopping a war is what I was sent here to do, and if I'm right, these different tribes won't team up enough to start one. And seeing as how my boss right now is the Indian Bureau, and that it's their job to see that the redskins' land ain't scalped off by a bunch of outlaw timber raiders, that's what my job here boils down to, and I ain't going to back away from it!"

Chapter 12

Standing at the upriver tip of the stretch of sandy soil along the riverbank, Longarm and Hudson had an unobscured view of the crowded crescent-shaped strip of the area beyond. They stood watching the activity in the clearing that ran back from the river's tumbling surface almost to the edge of the ragged array of little shanties that formed the Hoopa village.

Indians of the other coastal tribes had been arriving since late morning, and by now there were little clusters everywhere Longarm looked. Either by common consent or because the place had been designated as their meeting area, they had congregated on the beach, which was the only area in the vicinity that was not covered by chest-high scrubby brush from which the great trees of the redwood grove arose.

It was a large expanse, extending along almost a half mile of rocky riverbank. Accustomed as he was to seeing the Indians of the Rockies and the plains, whose garb and weapons had so many similarities, Longarm had trouble at first convincing himself that he was looking at Indians. In spite of their common origin, there were some startling differences in the appearances of those who came from the different tribes the gathering represented. The disparity of their dress amazed even Longarm.

Several of the groups were composed only of men, but in a few of the smaller clusters the number of women almost equalled that of the men. In a half dozen of the little bunches both men and women wore long deerskin or bark-fiber robes, in three or four the men wore nothing except loin clothes and the woman were garbed in long ankle-length robes.

More of the men had on breechclouts than robes, and those from a few of the tribes displayed ridged tattooed outlines of birds or fish or animals on their chests and occasionally on their shoulders and backs as well. A scattered handful of them had faces that were literally covered with tattoo marks, and there were two or three whose tattooing extended to their foreheads, chests, backs, arms, and legs.

One small party of men standing near the water's edge a bit apart from their fellows wore nothing except narrow belts made of strings of rawhide twisted together. Large knives in sheaths dangling from these belts completed their outfits.

Longarm could see painted faces in fewer than half of the groups. Among them there was one small group of four men clustering together who had their entire faces and chests down to the skin thongs that supported their loin-cloths painted a dull white. The painted area included their lips, which gave them the appearance of human trunks topped by fleshless rib cages and skulls. They were among the few who carried rifles.

On most of the Indians, however, the facial paint was

limited to one broad streak of a single color across their cheeks, or outlining their jawbones or their eyes or noses. In two of the larger bands the faces of the women as well as those of the men were painted.

After Longarm had completed his survey of the assembly he turned to Hudson and asked, "Do all them look like Indians to you?"

"I can't say they look like what I've always thought about as Indians. When you come right down to it, outside of these that're here now I haven't seen too many Indians anyplace," Hudson replied. "Except at one of the stands I worked on for a while. There'd almost always be a little bunch of Umpquahs hanging around."

"I never did see anything like this myself," Longarm said, shaking his head. "And I spent some pretty fair spells in the Indian Nation and a lot of other places where there's plenty of redskins, something like fifteen or twenty tribes."

"How many tribes do you think these Indians here have come from?" Hudson asked.

"Well, there's supposed to be about ten or a dozen from what Klalish told me, but I ain't sure there's all that many here," Longarm said. "I reckon the best thing we can do is see if we can find Klalish or old Viatsolof and ask them."

"I wouldn't know where to look for them in a bunch like this one," Hudson said. "There's an awful lot of redskins here."

"Come to think of it, I ain't seen Klalish or Viatsolof since I came down here. But they ought not be too hard to locate," Longarm said as he and Hudson began to scan the Indian visitors. "At least we've been around them long enough to pick 'em out of this crowd."

He'd barely finished speaking when Klalish's voice rose from behind them. "Oh, there you are, Longarm! I've been looking for you, but it's hard to find anybody in a crowd like this."

"Well, I sorta been looking for you, too," he said. "But I guess you've had your hands full."

"I certainly have! Some of the people here have had to travel a long way, and I wasn't really expecting them to show up. Now, if we can just get them to work together..." Her voice trailed off as she contemplated the problem.

"Don't worry," Longarm encouraged her. "I got a hunch you'll see everything work out, and it'll be worth all the time you've put in."

Klalish went on, "I'm not sure it will. I've been moving around from one bunch of people to the next one, trying to talk to a few of the headmen privately. I want to see how they feel about keeping the loggers out of our territory."

"I hope you heard some good news."

"Not always. Some of the tribes from farthest up the coast actually want the loggers to come up there. So do a couple of the inland tribes like the Wintu and the Chimariko. I'm sure you've noticed the Chimariko, they're the ones with their bodies painted white and their faces marked to look like skulls."

"It'd be awful hard not to see 'em. They stick out like a redwood tree would in a cabbage patch. I don't guess they got much to do with the ones along the coast?"

Klalish shook her head. "No. They're too far inland, so far that they're outside of the redwood stands. All they have is some stands of pine, and there are too many pine stands closer to the rivers and the coast."

"Don't they realize that even if the loggers did come into their territory they'd bring their own crews with them?" Hudson asked, frowning.

"No. All they've heard in that isolated area farther north is that a logging stand needs a lot of men to work it. They're thinking about jobs and money, not what logging will do to the places they call home."

"They don't cotton to your scheme, then?" Longarm asked.

Klalish shook her head. "Not yet. And I'm hoping they'll change their minds after they hear more, especially from the tribes to the south that've seen what happens when the timber cutters move in. But the reason I've come looking for you is to ask for some help in getting this scattered bunch together, at the middle of the spit, where it's widest. Will you and your friend give me a little help?"

"Sure. Just tell us what to do."

"You can see how these people are all spread out in little bunches," she said, indicating the open strip along the river. "If you'll just go around the edge and get them to move together at the place where it's widest, we can get the powwow started."

"We'll be glad to," Longarm offered. "But before we start, maybe you'll tell me how all this here mishmash of Indians is going to understand each other? Don't they all have different languages?"

"Oh, of course," Klalish replied. Then a smile formed on her broad face and she went on, "But all of us know enough English to get along, so it's become our common language."

"Now, that's the last thing that would've occurred to me," Longarm said. "Now, me and Charley'll get busy and do that little chore you wanted us to."

"I'll go back to Father, then," Klalish told him. Without waiting, she turned and started toward the center of the crowded sandspit.

Longarm stood watching her for a moment, then said to Hudson, "I guess we better get started getting these redskins herded up like she asked us to."

They reached the downriver end of the crescent-shaped spit, and Longarm said to Hudson, "Looks to me like the easiest way to do this is for one of us to go along the bank and the other one along the brush line and herd 'em ahead of us as best we can. You got any better ideas?"

Hudson shook his head. "I'll take the shore or the brush line, whichever you say."

"You're closest to the water, so why don't you just start along it, then," Longarm suggested. "I'll stay back by the trees as long as I can when the shore starts to widen out. We'll likely want to push toward each other about then."

"Suits me," Hudson agreed. "I guess they'll understand what we want them to do."

"I'd imagine so. Klalish says that most of 'em understand plain English."

"Let's go, then," Hudson said.

He suited action to his words by starting up the water's edge, calling to the Indians and gesturing in the direction of the sandy shoreline's center.

Longarm watched him for a moment, then began moving slowly forward himself. He took slow short steps, gesturing and pointing ahead, waving his arms to indicate that the small groups should move on ahead of him to the area where the crescent of sand widened.

Most of the Indians responded readily to his gestures. They showed no inclination to hurry, nor did they display any interest in those from other tribes who walked beside him. Now and then one of the little groups failed to respond and Longarm was forced to move close to them and try to convey by pointing and sweeping his arm in a semi-circle to indicate that he was asking them to join the general movement toward the broad area in the center of the sandy expanse.

As the distance between him and Hudson increased. Longarm looked across the widening expanse of sand occasionally to make sure that Hudson's advance was about the same as his own. He also stopped a time or two to crane his neck ahead and make sure that Klalish and Viatsolof were having an equally easy time in persuading the Indians from the opposite end of the sandspit to move.

Each time he glanced at the bobbing heads of the two slowly converging groups of Indians, he could see that those being urged ahead by Klalish were making at least as much progress as he and Hudson were. Apparently Klalish had been keeping track of Longarm's charges. She began pushing through the group moving ahead of her, and when she stepped onto the narrowing strip of beach she started signaling Longarm to halt his group.

There were several moments of confusion when the two converging parties met, a bit of pushing followed their merging and here and there some voices were raised in loud argument as old tribal enemies were brought together. By the time the small hubbub had subsided Klalish had taken the few steps necessary to reach Longarm.

"I want to talk to them a minute or two, and remind them that the trees growing on their reservations belong to the tribes and not to the loggers," she said. "Then if you'll tell them that—"

"Hold on, now!" Longarm interrupted. "I ain't a bit good at speeches!"

"You don't have to make a speech," Klalish assured him. "Just tell them that they've got the law on their side, and that when somebody starts cutting their trees down, they're entitled to be paid for them."

Little as the idea appealed to him, Longarm nodded. He said, "As long as you don't look for me to make no big long speech, I reckon I can tell 'em that much."

"We'll get started, then," Klalish said. Turning away from Longarm, she began calling, "Listen to me! I have things to tell you!"

A ripple of noise passed through the crowd, and there was a bit more shoving and jockeying for position. Klalish raised her voice and repeated her request for silence. Gradually, the Indians subsided.

"All of you know me," Klalish began. "And you know I will speak truth." A ripple of voices ran through the crowd, but Klalish did not give her listeners time to grow restive. She called loudly, "You must stay quiet and listen!" As the murmurs died away, she went on, "You know that white men have attacked our people, and they cut the big trees! The trees are ours, they belong to the people who live where they grow! Whoever cuts trees has to pay us for them!"

A voice from the crowd broke in, "How do we make them pay us? They say no pay, we say no cut, they cut anyway!"

"Then you must get the bureau agent to tell them!" Klalish said.

"Aie!" another of the Indians shouted. "Bureau don't make them pay! Bureau not ours, belongs to tree cutters!"

"There is a law!" Klalish called, turning in the direction from which the loud protester's voice had come. "White people's law! It says they must pay. Listen to this man! He will tell you this is true!" Turning to Longarm, she went on in her normal tone, "Go ahead, Longarm, say what I asked you to!"

Longarm had been racking his brain for the right words to use and had not anticipated being called on so soon. He opened his mouth to protest, to ask Klalish to give him more time in which to put his thoughts together, but when he looked at her and saw the worried frown that was on her face, he decided that he had no alternative but to speak at once.

"My name's Long!" he said, raising his voice above the murmurs and mutters and occasional shouts. "And I'm a deputy U.S. marshal! All I want to say is that what you just heard from Klalish is the right thing to do. If your Indian agent don't do what he's supposed to, you oughta hurry right away to the U.S. marshal and tell him! He'll see you get what's rightfully yours! And if—" Longarm broke off when a shout interrupted him.

"You lie!" the man's voice rose from somewhere in the crowd. "Tree cutters pay!"

"I never said all of 'em didn't pay!" Longarm replied. "I said if somebody tries to cheat you—"

"Tree cutters not cheat!" the speaker interrupted.

"Now, I ain't calling you a liar," Longarm said quickly. "But I know that there's some who's honest and some that's crooked, and I ain't—"

"You are who lies!" the speaker from the crowd broke in. "Tree cutters our friends! They buy trees, not steal!"

A chorus of voices rose from the men standing close to the one who'd spoken. From the moment he'd been interrupted, Longarm had been searching the crowd with his eyes, trying to locate the man who'd broken in on his words. When the man spoke this time, he spotted him as being one of the Indians that Klalish had identified as Chimarikos, whose faces were painted like skulls and whose torsos were covered with white pigment.

Longarm racked his brain, trying to think of a reply that would silence the protester without increasing the anger that the man was already showing. That the Indians in the vicinity of the shouting Chimariko would take his side instead of Longarm's was already apparent. Those nearest to the white-painted man were already stirring restlessly, pushing closer to him as though to assure him of their support.

"Let's stop this argument as fast as we can, Longarm," Klalish said. She spoke in a loud whisper, but her face showed her worry as well as did the tone of her voice. "I'd hate to see this break up because of a little disagreement!"

"So would I," Longarm assured her. He bent as close to

143

her as possible and lowered his voice as he went on, "I'll do the best I can to cut it short."

He straightened up, and looked toward the Chimarikos. They were beginning to push their way through the crowd. It was obvious that they were heading toward him. He leaned closer to Klalish and told her, "Looks like you got a few troublemakers. That bunch you was telling me about a minute ago, the ones that's all daubed up in white paint, they're the ones that began arguing, and they're pushing up to us pretty fast."

"Try not to make them angry, please, Longarm!" she said.

"I'll do the best I can," he promised. "But I don't think I oughta try to say more'n what I have already. It'd just make 'em madder'n they are now."

"Yes. I'll see if I can get them to be reasonable."

Klalish turned and scanned the crowd. Looking past her, Longarm could see the quartet of Chimarikos had almost reached them now. They were only a half dozen yards away, still pushing steadily in his direction.

Klalish had also located the white-painted quartet. She raised her voice again and called loudly, "Hush, all of you! There is more for us to powwow, then we will eat! Listen to me, all of you!"

Longarm had not taken his eyes off the four Chimarikos, who were still pushing their way toward him and Klalish. He leaned forward until his mouth was only an inch from her ear and said, "Them Chimarikos are right close now and getting closer all the time. Looks like they've just got one thing on their mind, and that's to start some kinda trouble."

"That's the last thing I want to happen!" she told him. "I don't know how I can stop it, though!"

"Maybe I can," Longarm told her. "But it don't look like there's much way to settle it peaceful. I seen it happen too many times. Now, I'll do what I can to stop them fellows without a fracas, but you better be ready, because I'd put a dollar up to a dime that they're bound and determined to stir up a ruckus, and the only way I can see for 'em to do it is to start a fight."

"You can't fight them!" Klalish objected. "There'd be four of them against you!"

"I'll figure a way to cut the odds if I can," Longarm promised. "This ain't the first time I've been in a corner. Just stand to one side, and I'll see what I can do to settle them down peaceful, but if I can't, there ain't nothing else to do but let the fur start flying!"

Chapter 13

"No, Longarm!" Klalish objected. "Let me go meet them and talk to them first. They will listen to me more readily than they will if you try to get them to do something."

As Klalish started to push and weave her way through the moving throng and raised her voice calling to the Chimarikos, Longarm turned back to Hudson and said in a loud whisper, "They ain't in much of a mind to pay heed to her."

"I can see that," Hudson said.

"We're going to have about as much chance as a turkey on Thanksgiving Day to get a bunch like this to agree on anything, once somebody's got 'em all riled up," Longarm said, frowning.

"You think there's going to be an argument?"

"Them four Chimarikos ain't here to listen. What they're setting out to do is to stir up a ruckus and break up this powwow."

"How do you figure that?" Hudson asked. "I thought this was going to be a peaceful powwow."

"It was. But I've seen the trick work before, when some greedy white man was after something that the redskins had."

"And the Indians ganged up on him?"

Longarm shook his head. "They took him on one at a time. Just as soon as one of 'em started to get tired he'd just step back and break away, and then one of the others'd move up and keep the fight going."

"And pretty soon the fellow got worn out, I suppose," Hudson said. "Well, with only one good leg I'm not much use as a fighter, but I'm ready to stand by you."

"I didn't figure you'd back away," Longarm told him. "But that'd still be two-on-one odds. If there's a way to settle this thing peaceful and not bust up Klalish's shindy, I'd sooner try and find it."

"How'd things work out at this powwow you were telling me about? We might get an idea from it," Hudson suggested.

"Oh, it wasn't such a much," Longarm replied. "The redskins made too much of the little trick they were pulling. I finally had to put a stop to it."

"And you didn't have to fight?"

"Oh, there was a little bit of a ruckus. But the Indians finally got what they were after. The confab busted up. As I recall, they were arguing about rangeland, but they'd do the same thing over water rights, or trees, like it is here."

"Even if I wasn't around when this fracas you're talking about took place, it's easy to understand," Hudson said. "But how are you going to stop them?"

Ignoring his companion's question, Longarm went on, "You stick around till we can see how this is gonna work out. If it looks like them skull-faced redskins are having any luck in starting a fracas, make a beeline to the shanty

148

and fetch our rifles. It might just be we'll need 'em."

"Two rifles aren't going to be much help to us with a crowd the size of this, if these Indians all stick together," Hudson pointed out.

"Maybe not," Longarm replied. "But if they see we've got rifles, it might help to settle things down." He stopped and frowned and went on, "And when I come to think of it, maybe it might not work out that way at all. Might be they'd listen better if we don't look like we're figuring on having trouble. Let's let the rifles stay in the cabin. We can get 'em in plenty of time if we see we're going to need 'em."

"I'll be ready to go after them if things get too rough," Hudson volunteered.

Longarm nodded, then went on, "There's just one chance I can see to settle things up without everybody getting into it."

"What's that?" Hudson asked.

This time Longarm did not reply. His attention was concentrated on the white-painted quartet. The Chimarikos had stopped and Klalish was still trying to get close enough to speak to them without shouting. He could see that her progress was going to be slow.

Finally Klalish and the Indians were only a few steps apart. The distance closed quickly and they stood face to face. Klalish began talking, but they did not reply. Instead they ignored her and began shoving away the other Indians who were close by until they'd formed a small square with Klalish penned into it.

Longarm saw her spread her arms, trying to bring them into a position where she could speak to all four at the same time, and he could also see her lips moving as she talked to them. Even at a distance he could tell that the Indians were paying no attention to her. They continued to talk between themselves for a few moments. Then the man who'd taken the lead pushed her away with a quick sweep of his forearm and with his friends continued moving forward.

Longarm stepped forward and began shouldering through the closely packed and restlessly moving throng of Indians that stood between him and the Chimarikos. Klalish was talking to one of the white-painted Indians, and Longarm assumed that the man to whom she was paying the most attention was the leader of the small group.

Suddenly the Chimariko with whom Klalish had been talking looked past her and saw Longarm advancing. He shouldered Klalish out of his path and stepped forward as Longarm came within a step or two of him.

"This woman tells me you say we come here to make trouble!" the Indian exclaimed. "You are who lies, not me! Tell all these people I do not lie, or I lose face!"

"We got us a standoff, then," Longarm told him. "If I do that, it's the same thing as telling 'em I'm a liar, and that'd make me lose face. Now, I ain't lying, and you know it! There's somebody that's primed you to come here and stir up a ruckus!"

"You lie again!" the Chimariko shouted.

Under the heavy coating of white pigment that covered his face, Longarm saw that the man's features were twisting with anger. He could also see that the Indian was trying to open a way to achieve his objective. Familiar with the ways of hostile Indians as he was, it was obvious to Longarm that the Chimariko was holding himself back from striking the first blow. His tactic was to taunt Longarm, trying to force him to lash out with a blow that would give the onlookers the impression that it was the white man who was the aggressor.

Longarm refused the bait. He said, "You came here looking to start a fight with somebody, that's easy enough to see."

"You lie!" the Chimariko exclaimed. "We have come in peace to the woman's *kalatch*."

"That's easy enough to say!" Longarm told him. "But if there's any lying being done, it's by you and them others with you, because it sure wasn't me."

Until now the Indian's hands had been dangling at his sides, his left hand holding his rifle by the throat of its stock. He brought up the weapon a few inches and then lowered it quickly. Longarm could see that his motion had been involuntary, not part of the man's plan.

Longarm had formed his own plan during the few moments he and the Chimariko had been sparring verbally. He knew the manner of thinking and the unwritten laws that were almost universal among the tribes. Gambling that the Chimarikos were not an exception, he wasted no time bringing his scheme to completion.

Keeping his gaze locked with the Indian's obsidian eyes, Longarm said, "You didn't set out to start trouble with me. I'd say that just about anybody would've suited you. Now that you see I ain't taking your bait, I guess you'll have to go find somebody else to try and fool with your trick. And when you try the same thing twice, it's you that'll lose face, not me!"

An angry growl rasped from the Chimariko's lips. He brought up his rifle, his hand still holding it by the stock throat. As he raised the weapon he twisted it to strike Longarm with the edge of the butt. Longarm brought up his forearm to shield his face and the rifle butt struck it with a muted thud.

When the blow landed, it was not hard enough to do any harm. Longarm's purpose from the first had been to taunt the angry Indian to strike him, for he knew the universal Indian code gave the choice of weapons to the man who received the first blow in a fight that grew out of a quarrel. He'd had more than enough time to tense the steel-like muscles of his forearm before the rounded edge of the rifle butt came down on it.

Longarm stepped back. "You got the fight you were looking for," he said calmly. He might have been telling the Chimariko the time of day.

"It is you who tricked me!" the Indian snarled. "But we will fight! And it will not end until you are dead on the ground at my feet! How do we fight, with guns or knives or clubs or with no weapons at all?"

Longarm's answer had been ready even before he'd prodded the Chimariko into the idea of fighting. He said, "I don't need anything but my bare hands to put you down. But if you feel like you got to have a knife or a gun to keep you from being afraid to stand up to me, I'll oblige you with whatever you fancy."

His voice raised, almost shouting, the Indian said, "I do not need a weapon!"

Even before he'd spoken he'd been handing his rifle to the man standing beside him, and before the last word of his bragging speech left his lips he was swinging his right arm, fist doubled, in a roundhouse blow intended to smash into Longarm's face. He did not begin his swing fast enough to catch Longarm off guard. The man's looping wallop ended with a thunk on Longarm's upraised forearm.

At the same time that he blocked the swing designed to put him down, Longarm was beginning his counterblow. It was a quick up-darting underhand jab, aimed at the Chimariko's chin. However, the Indian swung his torso, angling it as he moved to interpose his biceps and the bulge of his shoulder to catch the swinging fist and deflect it from its target. Longarm's knuckles skidded off the point of his shoulder.

Longarm's counterblow pulled him off balance when it failed to connect solidly, but he did not drop his guard completely as he felt himself losing control of his swaying move. He kept his fists up to protect his face and shuffled his feet quickly to regain his balance in spite of his awkward stance. The arching overhand swing of the Chimariko's tightly bunched knuckles failed to knock Longarm's rotating fists aside. The looping blow attempted by the Indian pulled the redman off balance, just as the missed swing had done to Longarm a moment earlier.

For the tick of a half dozen seconds the two antagonists stared at one another across the small space that now separated them. Longarm could see the Indian's eyes darting in quick flicks as he looked for an opening. For his part, Longarm was willing to let the other man carry the brunt of their battle. He'd learned long ago that a too-anxious opponent sometimes defeated himself by rushing an attack, trying to bring a fight to a quick conclusion.

Longarm did not back off, nor did he drop his guard as the Indian swayed from side to side, his eyes flicking in quick but cautious movements as he looked for a vulnerable spot in Longarm's defense. The Chimariko's eyes were burning, their black pupils almost lost in a closely woven network of red veins.

As Longarm watched the man narrowed his lids, and his fists began rotating again as he swayed to one side, whirled on a heel, and bent quickly, bringing up his clenched knuckles in a flurry of swift short blows while he lunged toward Longarm.

His haste to close in defeated the Indian's attack. As he swayed to one side, Longarm took a slanting half step and let the man pass him in a flurry of whirling fists. As the Indian's head came within reach, Longarm hammered it with a looping overhand blow with his right hand and a second quick short jab with his left. Both blows landed, the second reaching its target almost as soon as had the first.

Neither blow was especially powerful, but landing as they did such a few seconds apart made up for their lack of steam. Longarm's overhand swing landed squarely. It sent the Chimariko's head sharply downward where it met the hard knuckles of Longarm's left fist as it was darting upward.

Really staggered for the first time since their brief set-to had started, the Indian dropped his guard as he swayed, trying to stay on his feet. A babble of sound broke from the onlookers who were close enough to see the fracas in full detail.

Now the three Chimarikos who stood beyond their staggering chief stepped forward. All three were muttering angrily as they started toward Longarm, who was concentrating his attention on their leader. The Chimariko chief was recovering fast. He made an angry gesture toward his fellow tribesmen and spat out a few words in their guttural native tongue.

While the Indian was talking, Longarm was taking the half step forward that he needed to reach his adversary with his fists. He stopped short when the flat boom of a shotgun drowned the cries of the onlookers, and the smooth surface of the river bubbled when the pellets from the scattergun plopped into the water only a few yards from the edge of the bank.

Not only Longarm, but all those present swiveled toward the river, looking for the source of the shotgun's blast. For a moment Longarm did not believe what he was seeing. His jaw dropped, and the Colt he'd whipped from its holster sagged in his hand as he stared at the boat and the crew manning it.

Bull Kestell, the double-barreled shotgun he'd fired still angled in his hands, was half standing, half crouching in the prow of one of the sturdy oversized rowboats common to the rivers of California's north coast. Four other men—loggers by the look of them—were also in the boat. Two manned the oars, a third was at the tiller in the craft's stern, and another was standing in the stern close to the tiller.

Instead of a shotgun, the man in the stern held a rifle, which he had already shouldered and was now aiming. His cheek was cradled on the rifle's stock, his eyes on the gun's sights, the menacing muzzle slowly traversing the shoreline as he sought a target. Longarm suddenly found himself looking down the black muzzle of the weapon and dropped to one knee.

Before the rifleman could squeeze off his shot the bow of the boat caught on a submerged boulder and its prow rose high out of the water as the craft tilted precariously. The marksman with the rifle had not yet found Longarm in his sights. His trigger finger tightened involuntarily when the boat's bow rose in accompaniment to the scraping sound of its flat bottom grating across the submerged boulder and the shock of its impact registered on him.

Angrily, the rifle barked. The shot went wild. It whistled above the heads of the Indians milling around on the shore and thunked into the sandy soil well beyond the strip of cleared beach at the water's edge.

As the prow of the boat rose high above the surface of the water, Longarm saw his chance and took it. He squeezed off a shot and steadied his Colt for a second shot as his first slug plowed through the boat's side with a crackle of splintering wood. The men in the boat started the craft rocking as they scrambled to its bottom in an effort to find cover.

Longarm's second shot also tore through the boat's exposed gunwales. In the little craft, Bull Kestell was standing alone with his legs still outspread in the stance he'd taken when getting ready to fire. The rocking of the boat sent Kestell gyrating as he fought to regain his balance. He was swaying back and forth, waving his arms, one hand still grasping the rifle.

Frozen into the similar position he'd been forced to hold

when shooting, the rifleman in the stern was also struggling to stay on his feet, but the sudden change caused by the boat's collision was too much for him to overcome. He flopped backward, his rifle falling with a splash into the river.

Now all the Indians along the clear sandy riverside were milling, looking for a place where they would not be targets for the boat's snipers. Longarm's Chimariko adversary had regained his balance, but instead of pressing his attack he had half turned to look across the river at the boat. Now he barked a few guttural words of command and turned to race toward the river.

His three followers did not look back as they hurried to follow him. All four of the Chimarikos splashed in a ragged line through the shoreline's shallows until the bottom shelved under their churning feet, then they breasted the roiled current and started swimming toward the boat. In the little craft Longarm could see that Bull Kestell and his men had forgotten everything else in their efforts to stop the flow of water that was spurting in through the bullet holes.

Longarm did not bother to raise his Colt again. He watched Kestell and his three men stooping and swaying in the boat as they tried to staunch the streams of water. They were letting the heavy current sweep the craft downriver now.

All four of the Chimarikos were proving to be strong swimmers and the current favored them. They finally reached the boat and scrambled into it. However, Longarm saw as he watched that they had dropped their rifles at some point during their swim, and he breathed a silent sigh of relief at the reduction of the odds against him.

After watching for a moment, Longarm felt sure that the timber pirates had enough to keep them busy for the moment, and would not be able to mount another attack until they had repaired the damage to their craft and regained their composure. The little craft was rapidly being borne downriver by now, rocking and swirling around in the turbulent current. It reached a bend in the river and was lost to sight.

Longarm turned to Klalish and said, "Looks like you're rid of them for a while. But I'll tell you what, me and Charley will just take a little stroll along the river on this side of the bank and keep an eye out, in case they do come back."

"But you'll be putting yourselves in danger!" she protested quickly. "Surely they've had enough of a lesson!"

"Greedy folks never get enough of anything," Longarm told her. "And that Bull Kestell works for a bunch of greedy loggers. I was right surprised to see him here, because he was the boss of a redwood stand down by Humboldt Bay."

"But that's miles away!" Klalish protested.

"Sure. I ain't learned all there is to know about tree cutting, but I got an idea that it ain't such a much for a bunch of loggers to move to a new stand."

"That's right," Hudson seconded. "As soon as the big redwoods are cut and shipped, they move. And they almost always pick out a new place to set up a long time before they move."

"Stands to reason," Longarm agreed. "So we'll just follow them fellows along the shore and have us a look-see at whatever it is they're up to."

"If we're going after Kestell and his bunch, we'll need our rifles," Hudson said. "I'll go get them, then we can start."

"I go vith Longarm, too." Alexis Viatsolof's announcement took all three of them by surprise. They turned and saw the old man standing behind them. He'd obviously arrived while they were too engrossed to hear him approaching over the undercurrent of noises that the Indians were making. "I know vat country is like all over. If enemies ve find, ve keel them!"

Chapter 14

When Klalish heard her father announce his intention to join Longarm and Hudson, she exclaimed, "No, Father! You can't keep up with Longarm and his friend! Stay here with me, please!"

Without raising his voice above its usual conversational level, Viatsolof replied firmly, "They do not know country. I do. Veel go veeth them."

Though Longarm had no doubt that he'd be well able to find his own way, he realized that the old man could be very helpful in showing him shortcuts and bypaths. He also recognized that Viatsolof might be in danger if they caught up with Bull Kestell and his crew. He decided quickly that the advantages of having Viatsolof as a guide to the unknown terrain far outweighed the negatives that his presence might create.

"I'd be real proud to have your daddy go along with us, Klalish," Longarm replied. "And I'll see he gets back safe and sound, too. Besides, we're bound to catch up with

Kestell and that rascal bunch of his before we've gone very far. From the way I heard wood splinter when them shots I took landed, that boat they're in has got two pretty big holes in it. They'll have to stop and fix it right soon."

During the few minutes they'd been talking the noise of the crowd along the shore had grown louder. The Indians were now bunched together at the water's edge, peering downriver, even though the boat had long ago vanished from sight.

Klalish was suddenly aware that she needed to stay and reorganize the crowd she'd invited. Trying to hide her reluctance, she nodded.

"I can see where Father would be helpful," she said. "And I don't suppose he'll be in much greater danger than he is any other time when he goes out on those patrols that he insists on making. Just try to keep him from getting hurt."

"I'll keep an eye on him," Longarm promised.

Hudson returned carrying his rifle and Longarm's. He said, "I didn't try to bring anything except our guns." Fumbling in his pocket he took out a fistful of rifle ammunition and handed it to Longarm. "Figured we'd be wanting to move fast, and that means light loads, so I just brought enough shells to carry in our pockets."

Longarm took the rifle ammunition and stowed it away in his trousers pocket as he replied, "There wasn't all that many of 'em in the boat with Hudson, even counting the Chimarikos. And all four of them lost their rifles when they had to swim out and make that quick getaway."

"Move fast is best," Viatsolof put in. "River is too rough to go in boat veeth leaks."

"They can't have got too much of a lead on us," Longarm said. "And you're right about this damn river. It's rough as a cob. With the load that boat's got now, it's going to ship water pretty bad." Turning to the old Russian, he said, "They ain't going to get any too far. Where you reckon they'll put in to plug up their bullet holes?"

"Two places below vhere ve are is maybe vhere they stop," Viatsolof volunteered. "Both close, easy to get to. But ve must go soon, or they maybe go avay."

"All right," Longarm said. Cradling his Winchester in the crook of his elbow, he turned toward the riverbank.

"No! Here to start along bank is no good," Viatsolof said quickly. "River bends. Ve go straight, vait for boat it catch up to us."

"Now, that's the easy way to do it," Longarm said. "All right, Alex. You show us the way. Me and Charley will trail along right behind you."

"And I must see how much I can save of all the work I did getting this meeting put together," Klalish said. "I'll look for you men later."

From the downriver tip of the sandy beach, Viatsolof led Longarm and Hudson inland for a short distance, then turned to move parallel to the river once more. Soon after they'd changed direction the river itself could only be heard, not seen, for it was hidden by the thick-growing trees rising above the brush and vines between them and the bank.

Viatsolof set an easy pace as Longarm and Hudson followed him. They kept peering in the direction of the river as they moved, trying to sight it through the strip of trees and heavy brush. Now and then they caught a brief glimpse of its surface, dark and smooth, a somber greenish-black in the sections where the water was deepest. At times the surface roiled white and threw up a froth of bubbly foam where it shoaled over the many shallow stretches where big boulders and stones formed its bed on either side of the strip of rolling deep water that marked its main channel.

For the most part, the going was easy, though when they encountered the creeks they were forced to go upstream along the banks of the feeder streams to find safe sandy bottoms and avoid the flood strips. The strips were wide expanses of paper-thin dancing water flowing over the rocky bottoms, and in them head-sized stones covered with a film of moss were lurking to throw the unwary. The stones were kept bare of the stringy acquatic plants that might have provided sure footing. Their surfaces were exposed by the regular flooding of the little waterways during the rainy season, and were much too treacherous to cross.

Viatsolof's sure steps belied his age. The old man kept moving at a pace that pressed both Longarm and Hudson to match. They had been out of sight of the river for quite a while when Viatsolof halted at the edge of a grove of redwood trees. These trees were smaller in diameter at the ground level and did not tower to the heights that Longarm had noted in the groves farther south. A small creek— small by the standards of the redwood region—trickled along one side of the trees. They'd covered a fair distance at a good pace before Viatsolof called a halt.

"Ve resting now," he announced. He leaned his ancient muzzle loader against the nearest tree trunk and hunkered down with his back against the striated bark.

Hudson dropped to the ground beside another of the tall redwoods and stretched his peg leg out in front of him. "I been hoping for the last half mile that you'd call a halt," he said. "How much farther do you think we'll have to go to get ahead of that damn boat?"

Viatsolof shrugged. "Now ve go back to river along creek," he replied as he gestured toward the little stream. "Best place is they can feex boat is vhere creek go into big river. If men are not there, ve go across mouth from creek on shoal and stay close by vater. Leetle creek ve cross before ve get here is vhere maybe is they stop."

"You think we've already got far enough downriver for us to've gotten in front of 'em?" Longarm asked him. He'd taken out one of his long thin cigars and was striking a match. He puffed the cigar into a glow when he'd asked his question.

"Ven a boat is to leak, you got to feex," Viatsolof said. The lifting of his shoulders was reflected in the tone of his voice as he went on, "You don't feex, in bad current, rough vater, boat sink."

"You're right as rain about that," Hudson broke in.

As Hudson spoke, Viatsolof was rising to his feet. He gestured ahead and said, "Ve go more now. Is close."

"We'll be right behind you," Longarm told him. He looked at Hudson, who was levering himself to his feet, and dropped back to walk beside him as they followed the old Russian. After they'd covered a few steps he went on, "While we were walking up here, I was shaking around a few ideas in my head. You figure maybe Kestell's trying to cut a deal with them Chimarikos?"

"What kind of deal?" Hudson frowned.

"Why, to move up on whatever land that bunch of redskins has got hereabouts and start cutting trees off of it. He's got to have a new place to cut timber after his outfit gets through taking down whatever's left at the place where they're at now."

"That'd be a reason, all right," Hudson agreed. "It'd be just like that damned bunch Kestell's with to set up on an Indian reservation."

"I don't guess you've ever been over east as far as the Chimariko country?"

Hudson shook his head. "No. I've heard talk about it, but that's all. There's supposed to be some good stands of the little redwoods on it. And they're not on government land, they belong to the Chimarikos."

"Well, seeing as how I'm working for the Indian Bureau right now, and likely will be for a while longer, it's sorta up to me to see them Chimarikos gets a fair shake, even if they ain't the best-natured bunch of redskins I've run into."

"If anybody's ever got a fair shake from Kestell, I've never heard about it," Hudson said with a crooked grin.

Longarm nodded, then went on, "Soon as we get this mess here straightened out, I guess I better do a little moseying around, then. Because if—"

He broke off when Viatsolof turned and placed a forefinger across his lips and shook his head. Then he gestured with the rifle in his left hand, its muzzle sweeping in an arc to indicate the heavily bushed area ahead.

"Ve get close, now," he said, keeping his voice low. "Is only leetle vay to river."

Both Longarm and Hudson acknowledged the caution with a nod. They followed Viatsolof's example and moved more slowly, trying to avoid the close-spaced bushes as much as possible, watching the stretches of loose rocks underfoot that they were beginning to encounter now as they moved closer to the river. Within a few more minutes they began to hear the low-pitched chuckling noise made by its sweeping current, and with each careful step they took it grew louder.

Very soon now they came in sight of the river. Because the trees and brush extended to the water's edge, with only a narrow stretch of small boulders between land and water, they still had only a broken vista. There was no boat within their sight on the short stretch of shoreline that was now visible.

Viatsolof pointed upriver with the barrel of his ancient rifle. "Upriver is bend. Makes good place for feex boat. Ve maybe find them there."

They covered the few yards remaining between them and the river and walked slowly across the soggy moss-covered soil underfoot until they were at the point where earth and water met. At last they broke through the last line of brush and crossed a narrow soggy strip of vegetation-free ground. Viatsolof was in the lead. He started across the narrow brush-free stretch of yielding ground, but stopped and raised his outspread hand.

Longarm and Hudson stopped beside him. Now that there was no longer any brush ahead they could hear the distant voices of men, and the occasional thunk of wood against wood. Viatsolof motioned for them to come closer. Longarm and Hudson took the few short steps necessary to bring them abreast of him.

Viatsolof lifted his rifle and pointed upriver. Looking ahead, Longarm saw the bulky form of a large boat swinging in the current. Even though it was almost obscured by the brush growing on a spit of land that extended into the water, he could see that it was not the rowboat that Hudson had used in his attack. When a voice broke the stillness all three of them recognized it at once as Kestell's.

"No, damn it!" they heard the loggers' boss saying. "You try driving a piece that big into the damn split and what it's gonna do is make it split worse! Thin your splinter down some more!"

"If I do, it's gonna crack when we drive it in," a man's voice replied.

"Then we'll cut a fresh piece and start over!" Kestell snapped. "Now do what I say and don't take all day to do it! I wanta get back up there before all them redskins has left! They need the kinda lesson I aim to give 'em!"

A new voice broke the silence, saying, "Are you sure there ain't some way we can git the big boat farther on up this river, Bull? Seems to me that water's plenty deep."

"And I'm telling you again, there's rock reefs and shoals upriver that'll tear the bottom out if we try it!" Kestell replied. "We got to have the little one to go back in. I want them damn redskins to learn who's boss before we leave here!"

"All right!" the man who'd asked the question said.

"But it'd sure save time to steam upriver instead of rowing."

"When we get to working them redwood stands upriver, we'll take care of them shallow places with dynamite," Kestell told him. "But we can't do a thing until I wind up that deal we're making with the Chimarikos. Soon as it's settled, the damn river's ours, and we'll do what we please with it!"

The voice of the man to whom Kestell had spoken first called, "All right, Bull, I got that new piece of patching ready. You better come look while I fit it in, because I sure don't wanta have to do it over again this time!"

Gesturing upriver in the direction the voices came from, Viatsolof said, "There are the vuns ve look for."

"Sure is," Longarm agreed. "So let's just mosey up on 'em real quiet and see if we can change their minds about messing around here any longer."

"Ve shoot them?" the old man asked.

"That's gonna depend," Longarm said. "My job's to keep the peace and stop honest folks from being hurt. I can't just go around shooting wild and maybe killing somebody that's never even broke the law."

"Does that mean we can't shoot unless you shoot first, or tell us we can?" Hudson asked.

"That ain't what I said," Longarm replied. "Now, I got to tell them rascals I'm a law officer and give 'em a chance to obey the law and go away peaceful. If they don't, or if they go for their guns or start shooting, that's when we can start shooting back."

"Is better ve shoot first," Viatsolof muttered.

"Well, I ain't going to argue that," Longarm said. "But just because I got to hold my fire don't mean I got to act like a plumb damn jackass."

"What do you think we ought to do, then?" Hudson asked.

166

"I'll go ahead of you up the side of the river," Longarm replied. "Viatsolof, you keep right on the shoreline. Charley can go get into that brush between them trees and keep hid. I'll see how things look. You two have your guns ready. The first one of them timber pirates that lets off a shot at us, or even looks like he's going for a gun, you can start giving 'em whatever, and by then I'll be throwing lead at 'em, too."

Both Hudson and the old Russian acknowledged their understanding of Longarm's directions with nods. Hudson began picking his way slowly toward the brush, his progress impeded by the forest duff that the river's flooding during the rainy season left piled in riffles for a dozen yards beyond the water's edge.

Viatsolof made his way down to the edge of the soft yielding sand that stretched from the margin of the stream to the high-water mark. When he was within a pace or two of the water he looked back at Longarm and gestured toward the greenish water to indicate that he could go no farther without being troubled by having to pass across the yielding sand.

Longarm placed himself at the edge of the sandy riffles and gestured for them to start. He moved to keep abreast of them as they began their cautious advance along the riverbank. As they moved the bubbling of the stream grew louder, a signal that a stretch of rapids lay ahead.

They'd covered only a short distance when the stern of a small tugboat came into sight, bobbing and swaying in response to the swirling current. A man sat in the small space between the diminutive cabin and the paddle wheel. He held a rifle across his knees. Longarm held up his hand, fingers outspread, to signal his companions to stop.

He did not see Hudson when he glanced toward the trees, but noted that Viatsolof had halted at once. Spreading his palm, Longarm gestured to the ground in the universal signal to take cover. Viatsolof nodded, stopped his advance and dropped flat. Longarm went to his knees and leaned forward toward the river's edge in an effort to look ahead.

He found that he could see nothing through the brush, and left his rifle lying on the ground as he began worming ahead on his belly. He kept edging forward, and after he'd covered another short stretch he could see the tugboat clearly. It could have been a twin to any of the tugs he'd watched in Humboldt Bay while the *Ocean Gem* was heading toward Eureka after crossing the bar. The little vessel's single smokestack rose from a tiny boxlike cabin, the twin shafts of its pistons extended along the deck on each side of the cabin to the craft's single wide rear paddle wheel.

Before Longarm could move, the man sitting on the deck glanced up at the threadlike wisp of almost invisible smoke that blurred the clear air above the stack. He picked up a chunk of wood from the pile that stood on the cramped deck and disappeared into the cabin.

Longarm made good use of the time he now had. He rose to a crouch and ran, leaving his Winchester lying where he'd placed it. When he reached a point where he could hear the scramble of voices from beyond the tugboat's bulk, Longarm stopped again. The voices ahead were still undistinguishable, for a tapping of wood on wood began, making it impossible for him to separate words from the mixture of voices and the occasional loud rapping as well as the sounds made by the river.

He continued his slow advance, and after he'd gotten a half dozen paces farther a mixture of jumbled voices became audible above the tapping. Kestell's voice from beyond the tugboat was the first to reach Longarm's ears.

"You got it right this time!" the logger boss exclaimed. "Soon as the water gets to them patches you put in they're gonna swell and close up the split places. You men come give me and Shorty a hand!"

Longarm dropped flat the instant he realized that he'd stepped into a potential hornets' nest, for his advance had taken him to the point where he'd be seen instantly by the men working on the curving stretch of shoreline ahead.

However, he'd gained an important advantage in his move, for now he could see the big rowboat that had taken Bull Kestell and his men upriver to the Hoopa settlement. It was propped up on two large crisscrossed branches and Kestell was standing at the edge of the river. Strung out beside him four men dressed in logger's roughs were assembling beside the big boat. The Chimarikos who had fled earlier were nowhere in sight.

As Longarm watched, they began to work. Using long, trimmed branches as poles, the men started levering into the river the big rowboat that Kestell had been in when he and his cohorts broke up the meeting of the Indians.

When he glanced at the boat the loggers were putting into the river, Longarm saw the bright yellow gleam of newly worked wood on its sides, where patches had been placed to close the damage done where his Colt's bullets had shattered its planking. The men with the levers were moving the boat steadily toward the water. The clumsy craft splashed easily into the river, and for a few moments a garble of words and low-pitched calls of satisfaction filled the air ahead.

Kestell's voice overrode the lighter sounds as he called, "All right, you men! All of you except Jake's going along this time! Grab your rifles and come get in the boat, and then I'll give you your orders!"

The loggers showed little enthusiasm and moved slowly, some of them casting sidewise glances at Kestell, then picked up their rifles where they'd lain on the bank. The man who'd been holding the bow line dragged the big rowboat to the water's edge. For a moment the splashing of feet churned the water as Kestell's crew stepped across the narrow strip of water and levered into the boat, then Long-arm heard Kestell's words clearly again.

"We'll give the wood in that patch a few minutes in the water to swell up," the logger boss said. "Then we can go back upriver and finish the job we messed up. You men get ready. I don't aim to waste time. If we take on a little water we'll just have to bail till them patches get tight. And this trip we got enough rifles and pistols to give them damn redskins what for!"

Chapter 15

"I'd say we've got a right sizeable job cut out for us," Hudson commented.

He'd emerged from the brush near Longarm in time to see the heavily laden rowboat starting to move slowly up the river, two oarsmen on either side propelling it against the heavy current. While Hudson and Longarm were still standing watching the stern of the rowboat disappear around a bend in the stream, Viatsolof joined them.

When neither Longarm nor the old Russian commented on his remark, Hudson asked, "Think we can make it to the village before they do?"

"I ain't so sure," Longarm said. "We still got a chore that needs to be cleaned up here before we can take after that bunch of scoundrels."

"I forgot about the fellow in the tugboat," Hudson said. "What're we going to do with him? I just hope you don't plan to shoot him."

Longarm shook his head as he replied, "Killing a man

171

that ain't done me nor anybody else harm cuts against my grain. Likely that fellow won't put up much of a fight when he sees it's three on one. Let's just go back quietly and see if we can't tuck him away somehow so he can't give us any trouble."

They turned and walked quietly along the edge of the river to the tugboat. When they slowed down to make a final cautious approach they saw that the man left to guard it had dismissed any thoughts that he might be in a dangerous situation. He'd propped his legs up on the stern rail and was leaning back on the short bench in the craft's narrow stern. His eyes were closed, but his mouth was open, an occasional gasping snore bubbling from it.

Longarm pressed his forefinger across his lips to warn his companions to be quiet. Choosing his footing with care, he moved slowly to the water's edge and drew his Colt. The first intimation the sleeper had that he was in trouble came when Longarm leaned forward from the riverbank and pressed the muzzle to the dozing man's ear.

Startled by the sudden pressure of the revolver's cold muzzle, the boatman woke with a start. He reached involuntarily for the barrel of the Colt, but thought better of his move when his eyes shifted from the blued steel of the revolver and came to rest on Longarm's stern face.

Letting his hands fall, the boatman said, "I don't know who you are, and I'm not asking you but one thing. Just don't pull the trigger on me!"

"Don't worry about that," Longarm replied. "I'm a deputy U.S. marshal. I'm here right now on a little job for the Indian Bureau. As long as you don't put up no fight and do what I tell you to, you ain't going to get hurt."

"I ain't a damn fool, mister! I know when somebody's got me cold turkey. Now, you tell me what to do. I sure won't give you and your friends any trouble!"

Longarm removed the muzzle of his Colt from the boatman's ear and looked up at the thin thread of smoke coming from the little craft's smokestack.

"How long does it take you to get up a head of steam and start moving?" he asked.

Blinking in surprise at the question, the boatman stammered for a moment, then answered, "I got a good head up now. I can notch the bar and put out any time you say, upriver or down."

"If you could get this boat any farther along than you are right now, you'd've done it already," Longarm told him. "Now, I've learned enough about boats and rivers to know damn well them riffles a little ways ahead keep you from going any farther."

"I won't disagree with you," the boatman replied. "But maybe you'll tell me just what it is you do want."

"Okay, what I want you to do is open up whatever valve it takes to let off that head of steam, and while it's blowing you can be shoveling the fire outa your boiler and dumping it in the river."

"But, mister! Bull Kestell told me to keep a head of steam up, and be ready to move when him and the others get back!" the boatman protested. "It's a lot of work to—" His words died away when Longarm started to lift the Colt's muzzle again. He said, "I don't guess I've got much say about what I do."

"Not one bit," Longarm assured him. "Now get busy and do what I told you to."

Muttering under his breath, the boatman disappeared into the cabin of the little craft. A hissing sounded from the cabin and steam began shooting from a pipe that protruded from one side of it. Then metal clanged on metal and the man emerged from the cabin. He was toting a shovel piled with glowing coals. After a sidewise glance at Longarm on the deck and Hudson and Viatsolof on the bank, he dumped the coals over the side. A cloud of steam billowed over the river's surface as the coals hissed and sank out of sight.

Longarm glanced at the smokestack, where a trail of smoke still rose. He said, "Go on and finish the job, now. I ain't got much time to wait on you, so don't do no lally-gagging."

After the boatman had made two more trips, dumping a full shovel of coals each time, Longarm looked up at the boat's tall smokestack. Not even a tiny wisp of smoke came from it now. The hissing of steam had subsided several minutes earlier, and now only a few drops of water dribbled from the exhaust valve.

Longarm nodded with satisfaction, then said, "Now, just sit down and make yourself comfortable while we tie you up. We'll be sending your friends back pretty soon. They'll cut you loose and help you get your boat started again. If you know what's good for you, just take 'em right back to wherever they came from."

"Sure, whatever you say," the boatman said.

He sat down obediently while Longarm bound his hands and feet. With a final glance at the helpless boatman, Longarm stepped to shore and joined Hudson and Viatsolof.

"We lost a little time," he told them, "but I aim to give Bull Kestell a lesson that'll stick. Once he's had it, he won't likely be messing around up here for a good long spell."

"What've you got in mind?" Hudson asked.

"It took us quite a spell to get here, chasing all around Robin Hood's barn the way we did," Longarm replied. Then he turned to Viatsolof and asked, "Maybe you know a way that'll get us back to your place quicker?"

"Vy ve go so slow to here is because ve come long vay vhere is no trail through brush," the old soldier replied. "Now ve not vorry somebody see us, ve go easy vay. River

174

got much curves in it, boat go slow. Ve go by river trail, is straight."

Longarm frowned thoughtfully as he asked, "If we run into that boat Bull Kestell's in, you think we can move on past it without him and his men seeing us?"

"Da," Viatsolof said. "Ven ve see boat, ve go off trail little vay in brush, ve get in front from them, go back to trail, move fast, ve get there first."

"We'll have to shake a leg pretty good if we're going to beat Bull and his men to where Klalish and all them other Indians are," Longarm warned him.

"Da, we do it, but not if ve don't to move fast," the old man replied. "Ve go now?"

"Right this minute. And suppose you take the lead," Longarm suggested. "If we can manage to get ahead of their boat we can be back to your village soon enough to give them timber outlaws a big surprise."

Viatsolof nodded again and pointed away from the riverbank as he said, "Ve go little vay in brush, find trail."

"Charley and me will be right in back of you," Longarm promised. "Just start out and lead us to that trail."

Viatsolof bobbed his head before turning to the thick stand of low-growing brush that rose a short distance from the water's edge and extended to the point where it merged with the tall trees. Longarm and Hudson pushed through the heavy stand of undergrowth just behind him, retrieving Longarm's Winchester along the way. For the first few minutes the going was rough and slow, then Viatsolof turned upriver on a trail that led through the head-high brush.

Though the trail was narrow and seemed always to be leading them uphill, it was as well-defined as Viatsolof had promised. It was also reasonably straight, though there were stretches where it wove in and out between the trunks of the towering trees. In a few spots it led them across soggy ground where a spring bubbled up and purled along the forest duff in a narrow bed before being swallowed by the heavy brush.

They did not talk as they moved. Now and then they encountered boggy spots that spread out around an area where a tiny spring too small to burst through to the surface had softened the soil below the duff, and uncertain footing forced them to pick their way slowly and carefully. As they moved, Longarm tried to keep an eye on the river, but in spite of being able to hear the current's chuckling flow most of the time, he got only fleeting glimpses of the river's surface.

They'd neither seen nor heard any noises from the direction of the river that might give them a clue as to the location of the boat carrying Kestell and his gang of plug-uglies when Viatsolof stumbled and almost fell. Leaping forward, Longarm grabbed the old man's arm and held it, feeling its muscles trembling. He looked at Viatsolof's ashen face. It was very apparent that the old soldier was feeling the strain of the busy two days and night that had passed since Longarm's initial encounter with him. Viatsolof was leaning on his rifle now, panting heavily.

Longarm said, "You look like you're getting a mite winded. How about me carrying that rifle a spell?"

Drawing himself up to his full height, the old man stared for a moment, locking Longarm's eyes with his, and replied indignantly, "Nyet! Am soldier of czar! Soldiers do not geev up their guns!"

"I reckon you're right about that," Longarm said. "And from what I've seen of you, I bet you were a damn good soldier."

"You are soldier, too, vun time?" Viatsolof asked.

"Just for a little spell," Longarm answered.

"You make good vun, too," the Russian said. "I geev

176

you freedom from being prisoner, now. Ve are soldiers, ve fight side at side!"

"Well, thanks," Longarm replied. "But if you're feeling up to it by now, we better get moving again and not spend no more time palavering."

"Da! Ve go ahead, drive tree cutters avay!"

They started along the little trail again. Longarm took the lead and moved steadily along until they reached an expanse of rock-strewn ground where there was no cover near the river, and beyond it was what appeared as a form of solid granite. The river channel narrowed and the water ran deep and swift, its surface almost black, the current squeezed between the high rock walls.

Longarm had been shifting his eyes from the trail to the river and back. He glanced at the river again and saw the stern of the big rowboat disappearing around a bend only a half mile or so ahead. He turned and motioned for his companions to stop, then stepped back to join them.

"Looks like we finally found a place where we can catch them rascals," he said. "Their boat just went around that bend yonder." Turning to Viatsolof he asked, "How big of a sweep does it make before it swings back this way?"

"Not big," the old man answered. "Cliff go a mile from end of place vhere is big bend." He gestured to the slope behind them and said, "Here goes off." Then he pointed almost directly ahead and added, "There comes back."

Longarm nodded, then asked, "I'd guess there's a pretty good current going through the canyon?"

Viatsolof nodded. "Is narrow canyon, river run fast."

"Is there any cover along them rocks up ahead that we can use to keep from being sitting ducks?"

"At end of rocks is bushes," the old man replied. "Ve go straight, ve come to river past bend. Is little climb to go down, but is not bad."

"Then let's try it!" Longarm snapped. "If I go too fast, you just keep coming along."

As they started out again, Longarm no longer held himself back to make it easy for his companions to keep up with him. He struck out at full stride, and soon was a hundred yards ahead of them. He looked back now and then and saw them struggling to keep up, but the handicaps of Hudson's peg leg and Viatsolof's age were too much for them to overcome.

Reaching the top of the domed formation, Longarm stopped to study the terrain and to allow his companions to catch up with him. To his left he could see the line of the U-curved canyon through which the river ran, and he needed only a few quick flicks of his eyes to realize that the open end of the river's narrow horseshoe-shaped course was the ideal spot for the ambush he'd sketched to his companions. By now Hudson and Viatsolof had reached him.

"You say there ain't no cover along the shore," he said to Viatsolof. "But I figure that current's got to be right heavy in that canyon, so that them scoundrels are going to be working real hard on their oars. If we sorta spread out along the bank, we oughta be able to handle it."

"Ve move apart?" Viatsolof asked Longarm.

"Sure. I'll work straight ahead, you and Charley strike out upriver to where you'll be a little ways apart. They got us outgunned, but that boat makes a big target, and when I put them two holes in it they splintered out real bad. If all of us aim right at the front close to where it hits the water, we can likely put enough holes in it to make 'em turn tail. Now, let's go get set to give them rascals a hot lead welcome!"

Moving as fast as possible, they angled out as they made their careful way down the steep slope to the river. Hudson moved slowly, his peg leg hampering him, but he plugged along until he reached the final downslope. Viatsolof moved almost as slowly. Longarm was the first to reach the river, where it frothed with a singing current through its narrow bed between the steeply slanting rock walls.

"This looks good," Longarm said.

"Good for what?" Hudson asked.

"Good enough of a place to stop them timber pirates."

"Suppose they've already gotten to the Hoopa settlement?" Hudson frowned.

Viatsolof had been following their conversation carefully. He shook his head now as he said, "Nyet. If they there already, ve hear shootings."

"We'll just have to jump off that bridge when we get to it," Longarm replied. "And we'll all know what to do if they manage to get ashore."

"Da," Viatsolof agreed, "is good, your plan. Ve do it."

"I guess you know more about gunfights than I do," Hudson put in. "Let's go on, then. We'll do it like you said."

"Before they get here, we better go find a place where we'll have some cover," Longarm told them. "Let's push on and see what we can find along up ahead."

Angling away from one another as they moved, the three started looking for positions. Longarm watched them until his own descent down the domed formation hid them from him, then he concentrated on picking his way down the increasingly steep slope back to the river's edge. He reached it at last and looked upriver to check on his companions. He could see Hudson moving carefully downward, and after searching for a moment located Viatsolof, sliding on the seat of his pants down the last few yards that brought him to the edge of the river.

A shout from downstream drew Longarm's attention. He swiveled quickly and saw that what he'd hoped to avoid

179

had already happened. The big rowboat had rounded the river's bend, and to have spotted them so quickly Kestell must have been on the lookout for him. The current was swift and the boat was moving slowly as the paired oarsmen on each side of the craft bent to their jobs. Then Bull Kestell's brawny shoulders rose from the prow. He had a rifle in his hands and Longarm shouldered his own weapon without delay. Their shots blended. Rock flew behind Longarm as Kestell's slug went singing past him and splattered against the canyon's stone wall.

Kestell was ducking behind the high prow when Longarm's shot echoed the timber pirate's, and even over the constant song of the river the crackle of splintered wood was audible. Kestell rose from behind his barricade and the timber pirate triggered off his weapon. Again his slug whistled past Longarm to spatter on the rock wall, but Longarm stuck to his target and drilled his lead into the prow of the rowboat just at the waterline.

By now the plug-uglies of Kestell's gang were joining in the foray. The heads and shoulders of a pair of them popped up from the center of the boat. Their rifles were already shouldered, but Viatsolof's rifle boomed and one of the oarsmen amidships lurched into the second renegade. The oarsman jarred the rifleman just as the man was triggering a shot and his slug went wild.

Kestell reared up again. He was shouldering his rifle as he brought himself erect and now Longarm saw his chance and took it. He swung the muzzle of his Winchester, aiming more by instinct than reason. Kestell sought the shelter of the boat's gunwales too late. His brawny form jerked with the impact of Longarm's deadly lead, and the redwood raider slumped below the gunwales.

Upriver, Hudson fired and once more the sound of wood breaking reached Longarm's ears. Then Hudson's shot was echoed by the booming roar of Viatsolof's old flintlock. Its heavy slug tore big chunks of wood from the boat's bow.

By now the rowboat was spinning in the current. Suddenly the heads and shoulders of the two remaining plug-uglies disappeared. The oarsmen dived below the gunwales seconds later and the bow of the boat began shifting in the current.

Longarm fired once more, this time aiming at the gyrating craft's waterline. Again the noise of splintering wood broke the air. Hard on the heels of Hudson's shot was the unmistakable booming of Viatsolof's ancient weapon. This time the slug tore into the rowboat just at the waterline, and the heavy chunk of lead was followed by a shower of splinters as a long white gash appeared in the side planking.

Above the boat's side a fluttering strip of white cloth tied to a rifle barrel suddenly appeared. Longarm lowered his rifle and stood up. The man in the boat rose after a moment. He was still waving his improvised flag of truce.

"We're leaving!" he called. "Just don't kill no more of us or shoot any more holes in the boat!"

"Where's Kestell?" Longarm called back. "I want to hear him say that!"

"Bull ain't going to say nothing no more," the man said. "He's deader'n a doornail."

"Then you take a message to his boss!" Longarm shouted. "Tell him this part of redwood country don't welcome raiders!"

"I'll sure do that! And I'm one who ain't coming back here ever at all!"

Longarm, Hudson and Alex Viatsolof stood looking at the peaceful surface of the river. The sun was off the water now and the river was taking on the blackness of night.

"You vill stay vith us a vile, now?" Viatsolof asked.

"I can't," Longarm replied. "Because there's always bad folks that keep trying to take what ain't theirs. And I guess I oughta be glad, even if I ain't. If it wasn't for them, I'd have to go looking for another job, and I sorta got a hankering to keep the one I got now."

Watch for

LONGARM AND THE DEADLY JAILBREAK

133rd novel in the bold
LONGARM series from Jove

Coming in January!

LONGARM

Explore the exciting Old West with
one of the men who made it wild!